# BENJAMIN DOVE

Text copyright © 2006 Fridrik Erlings
First published in Great Britain in 2006
by Meadowside Children's Books, London UK.
This edition © 2007 by North-South Books Inc.

Published and distributed in the United States and Canada
by North-South Books Inc., an imprint of
NordSüd Verlag AG, Zürich, Switzerland.

Library of Congress Cataloging-in-Publication
Data is available.
A CIP catalogue record for this book is available from
The British Library.

ISBN-13: 978-0-7358-2149-1 / ISBN-10: 0-7358-2149-6 (paperback edition)

10 9 8 7 6 5 4 3 2 1

ISBN-13: 978-0-7358-2150-7 / ISBN-10: 0-7358-2150-X (trade edition)

10 9 8 7 6 5 4 3 2 1

www.northsouth.com

# BENJAMIN DOVE

F R I Ð R I K   E R L I N G S

WITHDRAWN

NORTHSOUTH
BOOKS
New York

*Reality is very different from adventures in books. In reality things happen unexpectedly, some wonderful and amusing, some horrible and tragic. But these are the things you remember, the things that change your life forever. And nothing will ever be the same. No adventure tale in a storybook can make that happen.*

*So maybe reality is the greatest adventure of all . . .*

1

MY PART OF TOWN was like a little world all of its own. And there all the adventures and mysteries took place that could happen in any world. There were also some rather special adventures and unusual mysteries that only happened there and nowhere else. All the same, my part of town was only a street and a path.

There I, Benjamin, lived in a three-storey block of flats facing the street. My friend Jeff lived on the floor above. Across the street, in a two-storey wooden house, lived Emmanuel, called Manny, with his mother and three-year-old sister.

Jeff and I were twelve and Manny nine. During winter we were together in school and in summertime we played together all day long. And even though the days are twice as long in summer as in winter, it was as though there was never enough time to play. Our mothers had to drag us home in the evenings and force us into bed. It was so unfair; practically bright daylight outside and there was so much we had to do.

Of course we weren't the only ones playing around in our part of town during the summer holidays. The bullies revelled in it too. In winter they often found it difficult to torment younger kids in the school yard and get away with it. But in summer it was as if these lower forms of life had broken loose from their fetters. They would dart out of hiding to torment and menace and scare.

In our part of town there were two bullies, Howard the Hood and Eddie the Turd. Obviously no one called Eddie 'Turd' to his face, and no one really knew how that handle got stuck to him. On the other hand, Howie's nickname was obvious. He always wore a black leather jacket and black trousers, and he was swarthy and had black hair as well. Some went so far as to say that even his soul was pitch-black.

The bullies were seldom on the prowl by day, so there was no reason to worry about their showing up until after dinner. And it so happened that it was in the evenings that most of the kids met up in one place in our part of town: the Ground.

During the day it was a supervised play-ground for nursery-school children, but in the evenings and on weekends we had the place to ourselves.

Sometimes there were fights, occasionally someone got hurt and not infrequently the bullies came to terrorise. And there were never any adults there to intervene if things got out of hand.

Except for Adele.

Her house stood just a stone's throw from

the Ground, behind the block of flats Jeff and I lived in. It was a little wooden house, clad with corrugated iron, painted blue with white window frames, standing in the middle of a pretty little garden with a couple of old trees and a white fence.

This was Old Adele's realm. She'd lived there as long as anyone could remember, and all the children called her Grandma Dell. She was the confidante of the housewives in our part of town, protector of animals and children. She never would listen when parents were complaining about our bad behavior.

'Children need to play,' she'd say. 'Don't forget that you were once behaving no better yourselves.'

Grandma Dell was the unofficial custodian of the Ground in the evenings and on weekends. And it was not unusual for a child to knock on her door to get a plaster or just a little comfort, a cup of cocoa and a piece of cake. She had a commanding view of the Ground from her kitchen window, and the bullies were never quite at ease going about their murky business, because of her.

Grandma Dell had the biggest cat ever seen in our part of town. It looked more like a lion's cub, sitting on its throne in the kitchen window, gazing indifferently at the world outside. She called it Socrates. It was hard to imagine that Socrates had ever been a defenseless little kitten, but Grandma Dell had saved him from a dustbin, when someone had tried to get rid of him. Maybe it was because of this experience that Socrates never showed anyone affection, except for Grandma Dell, for no one else was allowed to pat him or scratch him. He showed total disdain for humankind. Even when a big crowd of children was running back and forth on the Ground, he would walk slowly through and not move out of the way for anyone. And out of respect for this gargantuan beast, we would stop running and wait while His Majesty proceeded across the playground on his evening walk into the bright summer night.

2

BENJAMIN stands alone in an open field. In the far distance, majestic mountains soar up into the blue sky with their snowcapped peaks. Something is moving on the horizon; four horses are approaching at full gallop, their massive hooves pounding the earth without a sound. Four magnificent knights in shining armour sit astride, and as they draw closer they start to wave to him. Then he sees that he is one of them, another is Manny and the third is Jeff. But he doesn't recognise the fourth knight. They are shouting something to him, smiling and laughing, but he can't make out what they're saying. Suddenly they turn away, their cloaks billowing behind them like great wings. The earth begins to tremble under his feet. He tries to run, but he cannot move.

I woke up with a start and sat up in bed. Was I awake or still dreaming? The roaring I had heard in my dream surrounded me still. But when I woke a little more fully, I realised that a huge removal van was driving slowly past the house and down the street.

I threw off the covers and jumped out of bed. While I was dressing I tried to recall the strange dream. Something about horses? I couldn't remember anymore.

While I was eating breakfast the doorbell rang. Jeff stood in the hallway with a football under his arm.

'You just woke up?' he jeered.

'So?' I countered, pretending offence.

'What about our header competition?' he said, dribbling the ball.

'I'm coming,' I said, and put my trainers on.

As we ran down the stairs and out of the door he said, 'Sleepyhead!'

'And you're a Deadhead!' I yelled, and snatched the ball from him.

I ran towards the Ground, squeezed through a hole in the fence and dashed up the grassy hill. Then I kicked the ball high up into the air. Jeff came running, watching the ball falling, and got ready to head it before it hit the ground.

When there was just the two of us it was easiest to have a one-on-one heading competition. One stood up on the hill and kicked the ball high in the air while the other stood on the grass below and tried to keep it in the air by heading it. The kicker counted and we changed places after three turns. Jeff usually won. He was really good at this, running back and forth, keeping his eyes on the ball in the air. And because he was so good at it, he became very grouchy if he lost, so one really had to let him win a couple of times in a row.

From the hill, I could see between the houses and over the street beyond. The large removal van was parked on the corner, in front of the big house that had been empty for several weeks.

That house reminded me somehow of an abandoned castle with high, dense walls, the roof clad in green copper plates. The huge windows were painted white and the heavy double doors at the front of the house were embellished with elaborate carving and curved stained-glass windows. Big rowan trees spread their foliage over the roof.

'Are you falling asleep again?' Jeff yelled as the ball flew towards me. I just barely managed to catch it and kick it back into the air.

Two men in blue overalls were carrying furniture out of the van into the big house. I caught a glimpse of a huge chair, a throne really, with engraved arms and red velvet upholstery. On the high back was a carving like a coat of arms.

'Are you counting?' Jeff called.

'Twenty-five,' I said, just to say something.

'Bull! I must be up to forty by now!' he said, heading the ball into the air again and again.

'Uh-huh,' I muttered, distracted.

Finally the ball fell to the ground. Jeff moaned irritably and grabbed it.

'Someone's moving into the big house,' I said. 'Let's go and take a look.'

'But I had one turn left,' Jeff protested.

'So, we'll start again,' I said, and ran down the hill.

We stopped across the street from the great house and perched on a stone wall, watching the movers carry the furniture out of the van. All of it was in the same royal, grandiose style as the chair I had already seen—carved oak furniture, massive and heavy, which I'd never seen in any home here in our part of town.

Suddenly a boy in jeans and a jumper ran out the front door. He was tall and slender, with longish auburn hair that fell over his eyes. He ran around behind the van, picked up a big cardboard box and carried it to the house.

'Now, who is that?' Jeff whispered, wrinkling his brow so all the freckles scurried together in a knot on his nose.

I'd never seen the boy before, and yet I was sure I had; I just couldn't remember where or when.

He came out again and went around behind the van. Then he saw us, raised his hand in greeting and smiled.

I jumped off the stone wall.

'Want some help?' I asked.

'Sure,' he said, and I noted his strange accent. Jeff joined us and greeted him.

'I'm Jeff and this is Benjamin.'

'Hi, I'm Roland,' the boy said, brushing the hair from his eyes.

'Where are you from?' Jeff demanded.

'We're from Scotland,' he said.

'You're a McSomething, then?' Jeff said, grinning like an idiot.

'Yes, McIntosh, as it happens,' he said, and smiled.

I was feeling a bit awkward about Jeff's manners.

'So,' Jeff said, winking at me, 'you were living on Quality Street then?'

Jeff always had to go and say something stupid. But Roland just smiled, unruffled.

'Can we carry something for you?' I asked, to prevent any further embarrassment from Jeff.

We took one box apiece and carried each of them into the house. It was no less like a castle inside than from without; there was a huge fireplace in the living room, the handrail on the staircase was carved and shiny, the ceiling was beamed and the floor was clad in dark, wooden floorboards.

We helped Roland carry the boxes and smaller items, and his father and the moving men took the heavy things.

'Makes a difference to have such energetic helpers,' said Roland's father, patting us on the shoulders.

When the van was empty at last and everything had been brought inside, Roland's mother asked us into the kitchen. There we saw a frosty jug of orange juice and a plate of biscuits. Jeff and I sat down, but Roland hadn't come in yet.

'It's nice to see how you boys have welcomed Roland,' his mother said with a smile. 'New children are so often left out.'

She glanced down the hall to see if he was coming and added, as though talking to herself, 'It's so good for him to play with ordinary children.'

Jeff and I exchanged a glance but said nothing. We weren't quite sure whether she meant that we were ordinary children or that Roland was not. But we didn't spend much time thinking about that; mothers say so many cryptic things anyway.

3

I WAS CURIOUS to know what it was like in Scotland, but Roland didn't talk much about it. Somehow I got the feeling that he hadn't been happy there, and maybe that was the reason his mother was so pleased with us. Sometimes Roland talked like a grown-up. Once he said, 'Living in Scotland was tolerable, but I found it inadequate in certain particulars.'

Inadequate in certain particulars!

Was this what his mum was talking about when she said he wasn't ordinary? I don't know. But I thought he was a nice guy, at any rate.

◇   ◇   ◇

One day the three of us, Jeff, Manny and I, went over to ask Roland down to the beach with us. Manny had his little sister, Christina, in tow because he had to babysit her.

Down at the beach we built sand castles and dug a moat around them that the tide could fill. Naturally Jeff suggested a competition over which castle could stand longest once the water started to flow in. Roland and I built one, Jeff and Manny the other. Little Tina sat close by and played with seashells. As it happened, Jeff and Manny's castle collapsed first.

As usual when he lost a competition, Jeff started to complain, blaming Manny for not packing the sand well enough. But Manny didn't let it get to him. On the way home we took turns carrying Tina, who was fast asleep and encrusted with sand from head to toe.

After we had taken her home, Jeff suggested a football match. We wandered over to the Ground and sat on the grass while Jeff went home for the ball.

'He likes competing, that Jeff,' Roland said.

'Yes.' I nodded.

'And he can't stand to lose,' Manny added.

'Well then, he won't be disappointed with me,' said Roland. 'I know nothing about football.'

'That's all right,' Manny said with a grin, and the sun sparkled on his crooked front tooth. 'I'm hopeless too.'

'He likes winning,' I said. 'That's just the way he is.'

'It's not the goal that matters, but how you get there,' Roland said.

Manny and I exchanged glances out of the corners of our eyes. He certainly could make himself sound wise and philosophical.

Jeff came running onto the field with the ball in hand and took over. He decided that he and I should compete. Roland would be his goalie and Manny would be mine. The first one to score three goals continued playing, while the other changed places with his goalie, and so on.

Of course, I didn't believe that Roland

really meant what he said about knowing nothing about football. That's just something you say to play yourself down a bit, especially if you're very good at it. So Jeff and I scrimmaged fiercely, trying to impress Roland.

But Roland hardly moved in the goal and I soon managed to score. Jeff frowned and swore as he got the ball, and showed all kinds of fancy footwork before rushing to the goal, which Manny defended splendidly. Then I had the ball and I slipped past Jeff again and again, shot up the field and tucked the ball neatly into the goal, right beside Roland, who made a rather clumsy attempt to prevent it.

Jeff was becoming furious. He took all games so seriously. According to him, if you didn't know the rules, you shouldn't play. And it was usually he who set the rules.

I scored a third time, and then Roland had to go onto the field while Jeff guarded the goal.

As he jogged past me Jeff said, 'He's pathetic!'

'Relax,' I said. 'Maybe he's better than you think.'

But Roland wasn't. Jeff stood in the goal, shouting orders to him to do this, do that, to tackle me that way or this way. And while Roland was trying to figure out what Jeff meant, I snatched the ball from him and scored. Manny was laughing hysterically but Jeff was furious. He kicked the ball so hard that it soared over the fence and landed in the middle of the Ground.

Manny climbed the fence.

The ball was lying beside the wooden tower, standing tall at the centre of the Ground. As Manny bent over to pick up the ball, a black boot shot out from behind the tower, slapped down onto the ball and clamped it to the ground. Black leather trousers and a jacket followed, and suddenly the Hood materialised from behind the tower, with a loutish grin.

'Having a ball, are we?'

Manny froze and looked at us, terrified, but we just clung to the fence and watched. Howie bent over and snatched up the ball.

'Please let me have it,' Manny said.

From behind Howie appeared his shadow, Eddie the Turd.

'Hey, Eddie,' Howie said. 'He wants his ball back! What should we do about that?'

'Come and get it then,' Eddie said.

He took the ball from Howie, ran a short distance away and threw it back to him. It was clear that Manny was supposed to be the piggy in the middle, to run around and jump up and down, trying to get the ball. Just so they could have a good laugh at his expense. Eddie screeched, but Howie's laughter was a deep growl from the bottom of his gullet.

They kept on throwing the ball back and forth between them, laughing. Manny made a couple of hopeless lunges at it, and they just laughed all the more. Eddie tittered, Howie roared.

Suddenly Roland moved.

He jumped over the fence, strode determinedly across the playground and took position behind Howie, who was watching the ball sailing towards him. Just as he caught it, Roland stuck out his foot and tripped him. As Howie fell over backwards, Roland grabbed the ball and flung it over the fence, where Jeff grabbed it. We were ready to run away as fast as we could, but Roland stood stock still and waited for Howie to stand up.

He didn't have to wait very long. Howie jumped to his feet in a flash. He grabbed Roland by the neck of his shirt, twisting it hard, and bellowed, 'What the hell do you think you're doing?'

This must have been the first time anyone had ever attacked Howie unsolicited. Roland didn't move a muscle. He was perfectly calm. Manny edged, petrified, towards the fence, nearer to Jeff and me.

'I don't know who you are or what your name is,' said Roland. 'But you ought to know that only cowards make sport of picking on younger children.'

Howie gaped, dumbstruck, at him. He looked like those guys in comic strips who get hit in the mouth with a flying golf ball. Eddie moved closer.

'Who the hell do you think you are?' Howie finally yelled.

I'd never seen Howie angry. He was always cool and in command. And now here was some kid talking back to him, as though he took on Howie's kind every day.

'I'm not the one who thinks I'm something,' Roland snapped back at him. 'You are.'

Howie grabbed Roland harder and shook him as though trying to shake him apart, then tossed him into Eddie's grip.

'You asked for it,' Howie hissed.

Eddie shoved Roland back to Howie, who grabbed him in a headlock and dragged him over to the wooden tower.

'Gimme the rope, Eddie!'

From underneath his coat, Eddie produced a slender nylon rope. They tied Roland up at the base of the tower, with his arms and legs spread apart.

'Now you get to roast a little, my friend,'

Howie said, with an easy smile. 'Nobody mouths off at me.'

Eddie pulled out a flask of lighter fluid and squirted it all over Roland's jumper and trousers. Howie clicked his cigarette lighter and let the flames caress inches away from Roland's cheek, then down the length of his body, until finally the fluid caught the flame and part of his trousers were on fire.

'What's wrong?' Howie purred. 'Cat got your tongue?'

Eddie snickered in delight.

Everything happened so fast. We had been standing, paralysed, by the fence, but when we saw the fire crawl up Roland's trousers, we started to shout.

Then suddenly the shrill battle cry of an old lady filled the air; Grandma Dell came charging towards us with her broomstick held high.

'Leave him alone!' she cried. 'Get out of here!'

She stormed into the Ground, waving the

broomstick over her head like a berserk warrior with a battle-axe. Howie and Eddie looked up, as if unsure that this was a fight they could win.

'Grab the broom, Eddie!' Howie yelled.

Eddie tried to get the broomstick from Grandma Dell without really being rough. That was his undoing. She had raised three boys and knew how to handle naughty brats. She struck him such a mighty blow on the arm that he howled in pain.

'I've called the police!' she cried. 'This time you won't get away so easily!'

As if her words had magical powers, a police car careened down the path, sirens wailing, and braked so suddenly that the gravel sprayed in all directions. Howie and Eddie took to their heels and streaked across the playground towards the fence at the far end. They didn't seem to need to climb at all; they literally flew over it.

We rushed to Roland's side, shovelled gravel over his trousers to kill the flames and untied him, while the two policemen chased Howie and Eddie.

Roland stood up, rubbed his wrists and gave a little smile, as though nothing unusual had happened.

'Ugh, you stink,' Jeff said.

Grandma Dell came over to us, huffing and puffing.

'They'll pay for this, all right,' she said. 'Oh dear, your clothes are ruined!'

'It's nothing,' Roland said, looking down at himself. 'But I'd better go home and take a bath!'

'How did you dare to answer Howie back like that?' Jeff said, obviously impressed.

'Yeah! And without giving an inch!' Manny marvelled.

'I wasn't answering back,' Roland said, with a sudden spark in his eyes. 'I was just telling him the truth about himself. Howie is a coward. And like all cowards he hides behind his black armour of hate and violence.'

There was a moment's silence. We were

starting to get used to Roland's way of talking like a grown-up. But there was something in his words now that made me wonder who I really was.

I didn't do anything when Howie grabbed Roland, and neither did Jeff, who always acted like such a tough guy. It was obvious that Roland was hopeless at playing football, but he sure knew how to stand up for himself.

Watching Roland walk down the path to his home, he suddenly seemed so lonely. I wanted to run after him, walk him home, stay with him for a while, listen to him talk. Not just to comfort him; somehow I felt that if I had him by my side, I would be safe and nothing bad would happen.

But then Jeff punched me on the shoulder. 'Now,' he said. 'Let's play real football!'

4

SUNDAY AFTERNOON in Grandma Dell's kitchen, and the events of the day before were still shivering down our spines, although Roland looked calm and easy. Grandma Dell put a plate of biscuits, warm from the oven, on the table and poured milk into our glasses. Christina sat on the floor and munched a doughnut.

'Now, tell me something about your family, Roland,' Grandma Dell said.

'I'm descended from Scottish kings and knights,' Roland answered matter-of-factly.

'Is that so?' Grandma Dell murmured and sipped her coffee. 'Anyone really famous?' she added, giving us a wink.

'Well, my grandfather was Rufus Barebottom, who fought twenty Englishmen single-handedly.'

Jeff spewed his milk and I choked on my biscuit. Roland looked at us without smiling, as though he didn't understand what was so funny about having an ancestor named Barebottom.

'You don't say,' Grandma Dell replied, without batting an eyelid.

'My great-great-great-great-great grandfather'—Roland counted on his fingers—'was Robert the Bruce, King of Scotland.'

Jeff had caught his breath and managed to croak, 'Why on earth was your grandfather named Barebottom?'

'Well, that's obvious, isn't it?' Roland answered.

'No,' Jeff said. 'As it happens it isn't!'

'It was a nickname the English gave him as an insult.'

'Yes, but why?' Jeff cried.

'Well, because he didn't wear anything under his kilt.'

'What's a kilt?' Manny asked.

'It's a kind of a skirt,' Grandma Dell explained.

'Your grandfather wore skirts?' Manny asked, with a snort of laughter.

'You're making this up,' Jeff said.

'All men in Scotland wore kilts in those days,' said Roland, as though there couldn't be anything more normal. 'They still do, at festivals and formal occasions.'

'And no underwear?' Jeff cried.

'Of course not,' Roland answered calmly. 'That really would have been silly.'

We laughed heartily, mostly because Roland didn't realise how funny he sounded. Socrates sat by the kitchen window, seemingly unconcerned with the question of who wore skirts and why. The thrushes and starlings fluttering outside the window occupied all his attention. Roland and Grandma Dell talked about aunts and uncles from all over the country. The rest of us kept quiet and stuffed ourselves with delicious biscuits.

Finally, the biscuits were gone, and I could see that Jeff had grown bored of all this genealogy.

'Guys,' he barked all of a sudden. 'Let's go down to the shipyard.'

Manny glanced at his sister and then looked at us. Grandma Dell smiled.

'Run along boys. Tina can stay with me.'

Manny smiled his thanks, and we dashed out to the sunshine and the cheerful singing of birds. At the window, Socrates yawned like a lion and pretended he didn't notice us at all, as usual.

We decided to go fishing at the docks. But first we were going to show Roland our special hiding place in the shipyard.

The area around the shipyard was full of scrap iron, oil drums and various pieces of junk metal. For us, it was a haven. Our hiding place was an old van that was wedged into a huge junk pile, which stood on a low cliff just above the water. The double doors on the back of the van were our entrance, and apart from that you couldn't see the van at all.

Old Joe waved at us from his bulldozer. As usual on weekends, he was hauling scrap iron onto a lorry to be taken away. Joe lived right next to the shipyard and had worked there all his life. Now he was tinkering about there on weekends and in the evenings, just to kill time.

'You know, I will have to remove that one day,' he called as we ran to our hiding place. 'Don't get too comfortable there.'

'But it's our place, Joe,' I pleaded. 'Our very special secret hiding place!'

'Your hiding place, huh?' Joe said. 'Well, yours or not, this is my job.'

'We know, Joe,' Jeff added, 'but not today, please?'

Joe smiled and spat a foul stream of tobacco juice.

'Careful around the scrap,' he said. 'You scratch yourselves and you could get blood poisoning. And that's no joke!'

'Of course we'll be careful,' we called back.

Joe shook his head, muttering something, and limped away to his shed, where his coffeepot boiled with a whistle.

We were sure that Old Joe would never really get rid of our van.

We kept all kinds of things in that van, things that we had found on the beach or in the shipyard: a broken compass, old coffee canisters, a small anchor, a porthole window with a cracked glass, tons of bottles of all shapes and sizes. And it was here that we kept our fishing hooks and lines.

After we had shown Roland our hiding place, we took our fishing gear and went down to the docks. We spread out on the warm wood, put bait on the hooks and lowered them into the oily water.

The sun was warm and the seagulls circled lazily above our heads as we pulled the lines slowly, waiting for a nibble from a saithe or a plaice.

Finally Manny got one. It was a bullhead.

A plaice or saithe we'd keep, to give to Socrates. But a bullhead was a 'not to be kept'; it was ugly and had poisonous fins. The usual thing to do with a bullhead is to take it carefully off the hook, spit in its mouth and throw it far out in the water. We had learned that from the old sailors at the docks. And that's just what Manny did.

Roland watched him with a curious expression on his face.

'Why on earth did you do that for?' he asked.

'So it can't tell on us,' Manny answered.

'Tell? Tell what?' Roland enquired.

'Well . . . you know . . . that we're up here fishing,' Manny explained patiently.

'You're saying that you honestly believe they can communicate?' Roland asked.

Jeff and I convulsed and Manny roared with laughter.

'What's so funny?' Roland cried.

'You're just so incredibly serious, man,' Jeff laughed.

I felt a tug on my line and pulled it in. There was a glittering saithe wriggling on the hook. Manny grabbed it immediately, took it off the hook and held it to his face.

'Oh pray, inform us, Sir Saithe,' Manny mimicked Roland, 'and bring our debate to some conclusion; is there or isn't there communication of some sort in your most noble realm?'

Jeff and I were almost out of breath from laughter. The poor saithe was in the same condition, opening and closing its mouth, gasping for air. Manny moved it to his ear as if to hear better what the saithe was whispering.

'There is!' Manny shouted. 'Oh, thank you ever so much for the information, my dear Lord Saithe. But alas, I must tell you, your days are numbered. You are to be the dinner of that most noble creature, Socrates.'

I began to worry that Roland would be offended by Manny's imitation of him. But he was laughing so hard that the tears rolled down his cheeks.

What was so funny? Nothing really. But lying on the warm wooden docks with the sun high above and not a care in the world—that's paradise, that's happiness. We were laughing because we were friends; this silly laughter was our union of trust and friendship. And everything was funny—the gulls above our heads, the old sailors in the small fishing boats, Manny's crooked front tooth, Jeff's freckles, Roland's way of talking and the sound of my own laughter.

That's the way life ought to be always—happy, funny and carefree.

5

UP IN A DARK, wooden tower in the middle of the playground, a teenage boy dressed in black sits and fidgets with an old-fashioned cigarette lighter. He slouches and moulds his lankiness to the shape of his hiding place. He didn't dare to go home last night, in fear of the police. Much better to sleep here at the Ground, where no one will look for him.

Through a little crack in the tower wall, he sees the door of the house open. Four boys come running out, laughing. They head down the path and disappear between the trees. Their laughter fades away into the distance.

Then the old woman and a little girl appear

in the doorway. They walk hand in hand up the path in the opposite direction from the boys.

The boy blows a lock of black hair out of his eyes. All is silent except for the sleepy rustle of leaves in the trees nearby. Then he sees some movement at the window. It's a cat. A gigantic cat. The boy narrows his eyes, snaps the lighter shut and shoves it into his pocket. He stares at the cat through the slit in the tower wall.

The cat sits still in the window, watching the birds in the trees. He closes his eyes and yawns, not even bothering to kill the housefly that buzzes against the glass. He is falling asleep to her droning lullaby, when he hears crunching sounds on the gravel outside. He turns his head and opens his eyes. A young boy, dressed in black, is moving carefully across the path up to the house, swiftly but silently, almost like a cat.

*What curious behavior for a human.*

The boy pulls on a pair of thick, black

motorcycle gloves that reach to his elbows. The cat hears the door creak, and the hair on his spine rises. He turns to face the intruder, who steals into the house like a shadow, closing the door noiselessly behind him.

The boy has a thin string between his paws, stretching it with a funny sound, looking him straight in the eye. The cat bares his teeth and hisses, not sure if he should hide or attack. Humans are never to be trusted.

He jumps to one side and lands on the kitchen table, growling with fear and anger. A black glove grabs him by the nape of the neck, forcing his head down to the table. He claws wildly at the empty air; he snarls and whines and whips his tail furiously. He hits a sugar bowl, which rolls to the floor and shatters into a thousand pieces.

A noose of nylon twine slips over his head, and he makes a final, spitting, growling attempt to escape.

He hears the steady heartbeat of the kitchen clock on the wall, smells the familiar faint aroma of coffee in the air. A housefly drones a lullaby in the window. The string is tightened around his throat.

Then everything is silent and he swirls away into the velvet softness of a deep, peaceful sleep.

6

WE DIDN'T CATCH much on the dock, just laughed ourselves senseless. Then we got too hot and thirsty, so Roland invited us home for cold juice and biscuits. He showed us to his room and went to the kitchen.

This was like no boy's bedroom we had ever seen before. In the middle of the room was a small, round table made from dark wood, with four chairs. Against one wall stood a bed with a high, carved headboard. Wooden model ships hung from the ceiling, sailing ships with silk sails, twenty or thirty of them.

Beside a broad bookcase, which stretched from floor to ceiling, stood a large, oaken chest, and beside that was a great throne of a chair with red velvet upholstery and an engraved back. On the wall, next to the chair, hung a coat of arms: a winged red dragon breathing fire, standing on its hind legs and reaching out with its forelegs.

We stood for a while and took in the surroundings. Jeff walked slowly over to a large oil painting hanging beside the bed.

'There's something strange about this room,' Manny whispered.

'What do you mean?' I asked.

'I don't know. It's just sort of . . . creepy.'

'Look,' whispered Jeff.

We went over to the painting. It showed a young boy dressed in a tartan cloak and a kilt. On his head he was wearing a tasselled cap, and he had a pouch made of fur hanging from his waist. A sword hung by his side. His shoes were fastened with gold buckles and he wore knee-high socks.

'It's Roland,' Jeff whispered.

'N-o-o-o!' drawled Manny.

We were so transfixed by the painting that we didn't notice Roland enter until he put a jug of cold juice and a bowl of biscuits on the table.

'You like the painting?' he said.

'It's pretty . . . uh . . . pretty,' answered Manny shyly.

'It's fantastic,' Jeff said with a grin. 'Is that you in your Sunday skirt?'

I had hoped Jeff would keep his mouth shut, but of course he had to go and say something like that. Something that made you want to sink through the floor with embarrassment.

'No,' Roland said with a smile. 'That's my great grandfather, whom I am named after. It's his confirmation portrait, actually.'

I imagined having a portrait like that of my great grandfather, dressed as an Anglo-Saxon, or a Viking maybe! That would be something.

'He was the last knight in the family,' Roland added.

'A knight?' Manny whispered, wide eyed, and looked at the painting in admiration.

'A real knight?'

Roland nodded his head and walked over to the bookcase.

'Sit down and help yourselves; I'm going to show you something.'

He pulled a colossal book off the shelf and laid it on the table. It reminded me of an ancient Bible I had once seen in a museum; it had a thick leather cover with brass fittings at the corners, and was adorned with a beautifully engraved lock.

Roland opened it carefully and turned a few pages. They were thick and soft.

'This is the Family Chronicle,' he announced solemnly.

There was a large illustration of a knight in shining armour on a black horse, which was rearing up majestically on its hind legs. The knight had his sword drawn and his golden shield glittered. His crimson cloak swung out behind him like huge wings. He was one of Roland's ancestors.

Roland read aloud from the book, reciting tales of the valorous deeds of his forebears. Some had fought dragons and monsters; others saved princesses from evil spells or hopeless marriages. Many had done battle side by side with great kings of old in terrible wars, slashing on both sides with their sharp swords, spurring their horses onwards in huge battalions, with flags and pennants bearing the family coat of arms.

They had jousted and duelled with their enemies, sometimes to win the affection of a beautiful princess, sometimes to overthrow an evil prince. They had lived in magnificent castles perched on mountainsides with breathtaking views of their domain. In winter they sat in their huge banquet halls, feasting on venison and mead in front of giant fireplaces, listening to troubadours singing the poetry of fairy realms in ancient times.

Their weapons, shields and coats of mail, hung on the walls along with embroidered tapestries depicting their bold deeds. And despite all the battles and duels, they were all good and true knights with noble hearts, who fought the good fight for justice and against injustice to their dying day.

We sat as if in a trance, listening to Roland's passionate voice, and every word became an image in our minds. It was like watching a great movie, terrible, fascinating and heroic, and we lost all track of time.

Suddenly Manny jerked upright.

'Tina!' he said. 'I totally forgot about her!'

Instantly we were torn from the fairy-tale world of the great book. Roland closed it reverently and put it back on the shelf. We said good-bye to him and decided to meet again after supper.

As we turned onto the path, we saw Grandma Dell and Tina approaching the little house. Manny ran towards them.

'Oh, Manny,' Grandma Dell said. 'I went to

see my friend and got held up there. She needs to talk so much, poor thing. I was just on my way home. Have you been waiting for me?'

'No,' breathed Manny, relieved. He thanked her for babysitting Christina and then led his sister across the street. Jeff and I ran home; he continued up the stairs to the next floor and I went into our flat.

When I got into my room I opened the window. It was hot in there. On the table by the window lay my plastic knights, which I had been struggling to paint for some time. It was a fiddly job because every little detail had to be painted in the right colour and the brushes were tiny, with tips no thicker than an eyelash. I had finished three of them and had begun on the fourth, their leader.

While Mum and Dad were busy in the kitchen I sat down, with my head full of images of knighthood and cavalry, and continued to paint the leader with great care and attention.

Out of the corner of my eye I noticed some movement outside. I looked out the window.

Grandma Dell was standing outside her house, clasping her hands tightly together as if in prayer, sobbing. Through the open window I could hear her words:

'Help! Please help me!'

I stared at her for a bewildered second. Then I ran into the kitchen, where Mum was taking the fish off the stove and Dad was setting the table.

'Something's happened to Grandma Dell!' I cried.

They looked at each other and then again at me. But I was gone and dashed outside. Mum ran down the stairs behind me and out into the yard. When Grandma Dell saw us, she ran, sobbing, into my mother's arms.

'What has happened, my dear Grandma Dell?' my mother asked gently, stroking her silver hair. 'What is the matter?'

But the old woman couldn't speak. She pointed, trembling, at her little house. I had never dreamed that anything could frighten Grandma Dell. She hid her face in my mother's arms like a little child.

I ran towards the house.

'Benny, wait!' my mother cried. 'Benjamin!'

But I didn't listen to her. The front door was ajar. I entered cautiously and went into the kitchen. There was no one there. On the floor lay two overturned chairs and a broken sugar bowl. Socrates was hanging from the light fixture on a thin nylon string.

My mouth went dry and my eyes burned. I tried to move but I was rooted to the floor.

A warm breeze stole in through the open door behind me and stroked the cat's body gently, so it turned a little on the noose. I looked away, righted one of the chairs and stood up on it. I fumbled my pocketknife open with trembling fingers and grabbed the slippery twine just above Socrates's head, nearly dropping the concrete weight of him as I cut. I supported the dead bulk of his body with my other hand, stepped down from the chair and went outside.

In the yard a group of neighbours had gathered around Grandma Dell, who was still clinging to my mother. As I approached they drew aside, and I entered the circle with the cat in my arms. Grandma Dell turned towards me, weeping. She didn't see me; she didn't see anyone. She saw only Socrates. She dried her eyes and carefully took him from me, as though cradling an infant.

Jeff's father pushed his way through the circle to see what was going on. His face was grim, but then it turned into a mocking grin.

'Is that what all the fuss is about?'

Everyone pretended not to hear him.

Grandma Dell turned and trudged wearily towards her house. Suddenly she seemed so old, so tiny and fragile. I felt a jab of pain in my throat, a lump that stuck so firmly that it hurt. The group of people dispersed slowly and I was left alone in the yard.

'Benjamin, won't you come in now, dear?' my mother called gently from the door.

I was standing stiff, my fists clenched. I opened my hands and saw a trace of blood on them. I watched Grandma Dell disappear into the little house with her intolerable burden. My eyes filled, the lump cleared in my throat and everything dissolved in a mist of tears.

Under the bushes in the garden is a fresh hole in the ground. Around it are five people —an old woman and four boys. The woman kneels with a bundle in her arms, a cat's body shrouded in a white pillowcase. She lowers the corpse reverently into the grave. Sunlight filters down through the leaves onto the white linen.

The birds are silent today, as if they are paying their last respects at the funeral of their archenemy. Even your worst enemy deserves forgiveness when he is dead.

The boys stoop by the grave and carefully push the dark soil over the white linen. At last one of them takes a piece of sod and lays it over the soil. They have erected a headstone—a three-cornered slab of pavement stone. On it they have scratched:

'Socrates—the greatest cat in the world'

They stand silent for a moment until the old woman invites them inside for refreshments.

Manny is the last one to leave. He glances over his shoulder at the grave and wonders if flowers will grow there next summer. Buttercups, perhaps?

7

THE FLAMES stretched greedily up into the evening sky. Iron cables and rods were glowing in the flickering light, looking like snakes moving from side to side, getting ready to dart forward with their poisonous bites. The crackling of logs was the only sound in the quiet of the shipyard.

'Howie did it,' I said, still feeling the pain in my throat.

'Couldn't be anyone else,' Jeff agreed.

Then we fell silent. Roland said nothing. He just stood there and stared at the fire.

I couldn't stop thinking about Grandma

Dell. She was always helping us, helping everybody; she was always there for anyone who needed her. Now this had happened and what were we doing about it? Nothing. The burning stack of wood in front of our hiding place popped loudly, hissing and creaking with flying sparks and settling timber. I could feel the heat on my face, and it matched the burning wrath in my heart.

'Why don't we do something?' I cried. 'Why can't we do something for Grandma Dell?'

Jeff looked at me with a foolish grin.

'Like? The cat is dead, isn't it? We can't bring it back to life, can we?'

I jumped to my feet, furious.

'Of course we can't, you jerk!' I shouted. 'Why do you always have to say something so stupid? This is serious!'

Jeff stood up on the other side of the fire, pointing his finger at me.

'You just take it easy, now!'

I was in a fury. Jeff didn't understand me.

He never did. He was always making those idiotic remarks.

'There must be something we can do!' I continued. 'I mean, she's always doing things for us—for everyone. If she hadn't stopped Howie and Eddie the other day, they would have set Roland on fire. And we didn't lift a finger!'

'You could have,' Jeff barked. 'You just didn't have the guts!'

'Hey guys, stop shouting,' Manny pleaded.

He couldn't stand it when anyone argued. But I was boiling with anger at Jeff.

'So you're saying that *you* had the guts?' I shot back at Jeff. 'You're always playing the hero anyway. What stopped you this time?'

'Blaming everything on me now!' Jeff shouted, walking over to me. 'You're such a wimp!'

'You're no better,' I cried. 'We could have jumped them together and then none of this would have happened!'

I had worked myself up into such a lather, another word and I'd have started bawling.

And I didn't want that. I wanted to be tough and angry.

'So now everything is my fault?' Jeff shouted back. 'As if I killed that bloody cat?'

'Shut up!' I yelled in a trembling rage.

Roland stands still, watching the two boys argue, working themselves up to the edge of fighting. When they came to him this evening, grim and silent, asking him to come down to the shipyard with them, he knew something serious had happened. They wanted to include him, they trusted him. Now he is their friend.

He hasn't had many friends before; most kids tease him and call him weird, just because he isn't interested in football, running races and all the other kinds of sports that bore him to death.

No, he longs for the adventures he found in books, things that were real in the long-gone ages of his ancestors, the magical times of courage and chivalrous deeds.

That's the secret that he never dares tell anyone.

But now these boys are his friends. And they need his help. So he has brought his secret with him in a rucksack. They haven't asked about it and that's good, because he is going to take them by surprise. He will reveal his dream to them at exactly the right moment.

Jeff was shouting in my face, so I hit him in the chest, and in a moment we were pushing each other and fighting.

I heard Roland shouting at us to stop, and then his hand dragged me away from Jeff and he placed himself between us, holding us both at arm's length.

'Listen to me!' he said sternly. 'We certainly won't resurrect Socrates by arguing. And arguing won't help Grandma Dell either.'

He sounded like a teacher scolding a pair of nursery-school children.

'Benjamin's right,' he continued. 'We are worse than wimps if we can't help her when she is attacked. But we can help her only if we stand together. If we intend never to let Howie and Eddie get away with this behavior again, against us or anyone, then we have to stand together, as a team, as friends.'

Jeff and I eyed each other. I felt like a fool and sat down by the fire. So did Jeff. Manny breathed out, relieved that the fight was over. Roland turned away and picked up the big rucksack he had brought along with him. I hadn't noticed it until now. He studied us for a moment.

'Are you leaving?' Manny asked.

'Wait here a minute,' Roland answered. Then he vanished into the dark beyond the fire.

Jeff and I didn't look at each other for a while. Then I decided to break the ice and sighed.

'I'm sorry, Jeff,' I said lamely.

'It's all right,' he said, and grinned sheepishly.

'Roland is right, you know,' Manny said, poking the fire with a stick. 'We have to stand together.'

Jeff looked blankly at him and said with

a shrug, 'Stand together? What for? To do what?'

Moments went by in silence, broken only by the cracking and popping of the wood as it was consumed by the flames.

Then we heard a rattling sound from the junk pile behind us. We whirled around and there he stood, on the roof of our hiding place. The flames threw their uncanny flickering light at him as he loomed above us with a metal helmet on his head.

The shield in his left hand glittered like gold in the firelight, and on the breast of his tunic a fierce red dragon leaped on a white background. His vermillion cloak flowed elegantly to his ankles. His right hand raised a large sword as he shouted above the crackling of the fire.

'I am Roland! A Knight of the Order of the Red Dragon! I fight for justice, against injustice! Is there anyone here who will follow me?'

His words reverberated in the silence of

the shipyard, like a recruiting call from ancient times. Suddenly the tension within us snapped and flowed like an electric current down to our fingertips. We stood there, three boys by the fire, looking at him, our leader, raising his sword, calling us to arms.

'I will! I will! I will!' we shouted as one. 'For justice! Against injustice!'

We danced crazily around the fire, shouting until the entire shipyard echoed our litanies.

Knights! We would be real knights! With swords and shields and capes and helmets! We'd be invincible, and no one could defeat us, as long as we stood together, one for all, and all for one!

For justice, against injustice!

8

ROLAND'S garage became our armoury. We made shields from plywood, sawing, nailing, gluing and varnishing, until they were ready for painting. We changed innocent-looking paint cans into shining helmets, hammering wildly, bending and bashing them, sanding and polishing. The swords were tricky because first we had to whittle the blades and file them smooth, which was more tedious and time consuming than we'd guessed. The hilts we crafted individually too, so that each of us had his own special shape.

For three whole days we sweated in the garage when every normal kid in our part of town was playing football or hide-and-seek, bicycling or just enjoying the warm summer days. But we had a serious mission and it was no game. This was for real.

Manny's mother got stuck with sewing our capes and vests. We had to produce the fabric ourselves, however, and that proved a real test of our ingenuity. Jeff, who had to have everything classiest, didn't give up pestering his mother until she agreed to take him to a shop and buy material for his cape. He wasn't satisfied until he'd got a fur collar for it. Then he found an old chair in the basement, from which he took the leather seat cover for his vest. Manny's poor mother slaved for days, wrestling with its creation.

My cape was made from old silver-grey curtains with a brocaded design. The curtains had once hung in our living room, so there was enough material for a vest as well. Manny's cape was a deep scarlet with gold trim, and his vest was of multicoloured velvet in a diamond-shaped pattern.

While Manny's mum was doing the sewing, we leafed through books at Roland's round table, looking for heraldic symbols to paint on our shields. Jeff couldn't make up his mind whether he wanted a roaring winged lion or a black panther with fiery glowing eyes. In the end he settled on a double-headed eagle, black on a red background, with spreading wings and sharp claws.

Manny chose a white unicorn on a blue background. The strange thing was that Manny was rather scared of horses. When he was little he had been put astride a horse and had been really terrified.

'But they're very beautiful, and unicorns especially,' he said fondly. 'They are kind, and the most powerful of all. They're the kings of horses.'

I chose a white dove on a dark-grey background.

It was a solemn group of knights that posed, three days later, in front of the big mirror in Manny's house, dressed in our costumes, wooden swords at our sides and shields in hand. It was a moment full of deep meaning that we could feel but not explain. This wasn't just a game; behind these uniforms and weapons lay a holy purpose, an unwavering commitment: for justice, against injustice. And in the mirror we saw this commitment realised. We were knights, warriors of righteousness, ready for battle.

Back in Roland's room we gathered at the round table. Side by side on the wall behind us hung our helmets and weapons. In the Knights' Chamber everything was ready for the first meeting of the Order of the Red Dragon.

'Benjamin Dove,' announced Roland. 'I designate you Secretary of the Order. Your duty is to keep the minutes, to make written record of all decisions made at meetings and to record a description of all operational tactics employed by the Order.'

I was prepared for this position and had

bought a little book, leather bound with yellow pages. On the title page I had drawn the coat of arms of the Order, the Red Dragon, and underneath I had drawn each of our individual insignia and written our names: Roland Dragon, Benjamin Dove, Jeff Eagle, Manny Unicorn.

'Our first item is Howie the Hood,' said Roland. 'How shall we avenge Socrates? How shall Howie pay for his misdeeds?'

We looked at each other for a moment, each obviously contemplating various methods of torturing Howie the Hood. But Jeff was the one to voice his thoughts.

'If he only had a dog or some other pet that we could kill,' he said, with a bloodthirsty gleam in his eye.

'No,' Roland said. 'That wouldn't do at all.'

'Why not?' Jeff replied. 'It would be just payback for what he did to Grandma Dell.'

Something harsh in the tone of his voice made me vaguely uneasy.

'Naturally, you can see for yourself that that's impossible,' said Roland.

'Why?' Jeff demanded.

'Wouldn't that make us just as bad as him?' Manny said.

'Killing an innocent animal is not just in this case—nor any case, for that matter,' Roland said.

Jeff shrugged his shoulders and sighed.

'Like I said,' he mumbled. 'Howie doesn't have any pets anyway.'

'On the other hand,' Roland continued, 'we could do something to him, something to make him remember that evil deeds exact their punishment. We could do something so catastrophic that he'll never forget it.'

Manny and I nodded and smiled.

'I suggest,' said Roland, 'that we go on a reconnaissance mission to Howie's house late this evening. We have to survey the entire situation and find the weak spot in our enemy's armour. Agreed?'

Everyone raised a hand.

'All right. Then we meet again, here at my house, at nine o'clock this evening. But next on the agenda,' Roland said with a smile, 'is fencing practice!'

'Great!' Jeff cried, back to his old self again. 'Let's get going!'

We rushed to our feet, put on our capes and fastened our swords at our waists.

'Onward, men!' Jeff shouted with a dramatic wave of his sword.

We swarmed up the street, our capes taking flight behind us, the sun glittering on our shields and helmets. The excitement of upcoming adventures enveloped us.

Over at the Ground the youngest children were playing in the sandbox and nursery-school teachers were running around blowing noses and drying tears, while the older kids amused themselves on the swings and the see-saws. As we stormed onto the grass beside the playground, looking like a band of ancient heroes, the chatter of the children dropped into abrupt silence. They probably thought we were putting on a play for them. The teachers smiled at each other, but we pretended to see no one. On top of the hill, Roland planted a flagpole with a white banner bearing the Red Dragon. We took position around it, unsheathed our swords and saluted the flag.

'We begin in pairs,' said Roland. 'I against Benjamin Dove, Jeff Eagle against Manny Unicorn. You're not allowed to hit in the face or stab in the stomach. If the swords gets behind the opponent's shield, then that's a point, unless the opponent parries with his sword. Three points constitute a victory. So, let us begin!'

We positioned ourselves with drawn swords, and when Roland gave the signal we started fencing. The children in the playground lined up by the fence that separated their field from ours, excitedly watching our every move.

We began cautiously. The swords fitted our palms like a handshake; our shields were light and strong. Gradually our confidence grew; I advanced and retreated, parrying deftly, switching from defence to attack, feigning a jab to my opponent's arm, then changing direction with lightning speed and hitting his ankle.

'One point!' I called, and Roland acknowledged that.

On the path a group of children from our part of town was assembling to watch the spectacle. They started to cheer us on: 'Come on, Eagle! Get him, Dragon! Good move, Dove! Go for it, Unicorn!'

We were flushed with excitement. Our strokes became sharper and more confident; our capes flew as our swords split the air. We danced back and forth on the field to the percussive clatter and clang of sword meeting shield.

Roland was better than I was. I only managed to score one point against him, but he scored twice against me, and then gained the winning third point. We paused to catch our breath and watched Jeff and Manny fight. I had thought they would be mismatched because Manny was so much smaller than

Jeff. But he was quick and light on his feet, whereas Jeff was heavier and slower.

Several times Manny jumped unexpectedly to one side, so Jeff's heavy slashes missed their mark. Then all at once Manny advanced and cornered Jeff, who barely managed to raise his shield in defence.

I saw that Jeff was furious. He couldn't stand to lose. He had to have the upper hand.

'Go, Unicorn!' cheered the crowd of onlookers.

Manny had now penetrated Jeff's defence twice, and then Jeff scored his second point. He drove his sword with all his might into Manny's chest, and Manny nearly fell backwards from the force of it. Jeff advanced closer, and Manny stepped on his own cape and fell flat on his back. Instead of helping him to his feet, Jeff raised his sword menacingly. Manny rolled aside, just before the blow fell.

'Yes! Unicorn!' the crowd screamed delightedly.

The score was tied, two-two. I glanced at

Roland and noticed that he was watching Jeff with a worried frown. It was obvious that Jeff was fighting in anger. Manny had won over the crowd, and Jeff couldn't tolerate that. He had to win, so everyone could see that he was the best. That bighead. He always had to take everything so seriously.

Roland was about to stand up and call off the match when Manny ducked suddenly, put his shield above his head and delivered a nimble jab into Jeff's side.

'Three points for Emmanuel Unicorn!' Roland shouted.

The crowed whistled and applauded. Manny threw himself on the grass, panting, with a big smile on his face.

Jeff stood aside and gritted his teeth, his eyes darting at the dispersing crowd. Roland and I stood up and took the flagpole down.

'That was a fine match, Manny,' Roland said, clapping his hands and walking down the hill towards them.

I could see a burning flame in Jeff's eyes.

Suddenly he snapped out of his smouldering stupor. He jumped at Manny, sword aloft, and cracked him a solid blow across the chest Manny yelped and rolled over, writhing in pain.

I ran down the hill, knelt by his side and turned him gently. The blow had hit him on the ribs and shoulder. He tried hard to swallow the pain, but the tears were running down his cheeks. I could hear Roland talking to Jeff.

'What's the matter with you? This is practice, not a battle. Must you behave like a savage?'

'But I won!' Jeff insisted. There was that hard edge in his voice again. 'He only hit me twice!'

'He hit you three times. I saw it,' Roland replied.

'How could you see? You were up there,' Jeff said and pointed his sword to the hill.

'I was watching very carefully,' Roland said. 'But that is not the point, is it? You didn't have to hurt him!'

'Bah! It's nothing,' Jeff said, turning to Manny. 'That didn't hurt, did it?'

Manny looked away and dried his eyes

quickly. Then he stood up slowly, rubbing his shoulder. Jeff walked over to him and clapped him jovially on the back.

'See! He's not hurt!'

Manny glanced at him but didn't say anything.

'Well, if I hurt you I didn't mean to,' Jeff added. 'Maybe my sword is a bit too heavy though.'

He grinned, cutting the air around him several times, weighing the sword in his hand.

The spectators had begun to drift away, and the little children had long since resumed their play. I saw my mother standing by a window, waving at me.

'I've got to go in for supper,' I said.

'Nine o'clock at my house, then,' Roland reminded us.

At the corner Manny said good-bye in a low voice and ran across the street. I couldn't help noticing that he was crying.

Jeff followed me into our block of flats. I didn't want to speak, but he turned to me on the staircase.

'He only hit me twice, you know. It was I who won.'

I hesitated with my hand on the door to my flat. Was he really expecting me to agree with his violence? He stood on the staircase above me, staring at me with a stubborn look on his face. Usually I agreed when Jeff insisted on being right, just to avoid a tiresome argument. But not now. I couldn't bring myself to answer him, because I knew he would just become more and more certain that I was wrong and he was right.

*You're wrong*, I thought, but didn't say anything. A shadow moved across his face. He had heard my thoughts. And he ran upstairs.

Jeff Eagle, a brave Knight of the Order of the Red Dragon, storms into his flat, slamming the door behind him.

'What the hell is going on?' his father shouts from the living room. Jeff enters the room, unsheathes his sword proudly and shows it to his father.

'I beat them all, Dad. I fought all three and beat them all! It was quite a fight.'

His father lowers the newspaper for a second and looks at him.

'What's the meaning of this dress? Have you finally gone mad?'

He glances at the sword with a frown, and then points at the shield with a grin.

'There's no such thing as a bird with two heads.'

'It's a kind of symbol, Dad, you know, a coat of arms.'

'Well, don't go waving that thing in here, you hear me!' his father says, raising his newspaper again.

'See that mark here, Dad,' Jeff says, pointing eagerly at a scratch on his sword. 'This came when I broke Roland's shield in a single blow!'

'Jesus, boy! Didn't you hear me?' his father shouts from behind the paper. 'In your room with that junk or you'll feel the back of my hand!'

On the way to his room he walks past a

full-length mirror. He sees his reflection, but he doesn't recognise that angry face, those cold eyes. Then he raises the sword so the tip touches the mirror lightly. On the shield are the scars of battle. His armour is tough and strong; thick leather vest, heavy sword, strong shield. He is tough and strong. And he won. He is victorious. Invincible.

In the kitchen of the little house across the street, a young knight is buttering bread for his little sister. He sniffs and dries his tears on his sleeve. His mother just called; she's working late, so he has to babysit. It means he won't be able to go with the boys tonight. For the first time he is relieved just to stay home. He doesn't want the others to see he's been crying. He tried not to, but the blow was so sharp.

*I'll call Benjamin*, he thinks, *and tell him I can't make it tonight.* He goes into the bathroom and takes off his jumper. There's a red stripe on his chest, and his shoulder aches miserably.

*No, I will call Jeff. Then they'll never say I'm a wimp, just because I'm the youngest.*

He picks up the phone and dials. Asks for Jeff.

'Hi, man. What a fight, huh? Nah, doesn't hurt a bit. Not even a scratch. I can't come tonight; I've got to babysit. Mum's working late. Yeah, what a drag. You tell the others, all right? Yep, see you tomorrow.'

He hangs up the phone. Invincible.

9

THROUGH THE tangle of berry bushes, our eyes followed everything that happened in the house. It was a wooden house, sided with battered and rusty corrugated iron, set in a nasty neighbourhood of similar houses. A light shone on the first floor, for there were no curtains at the two windows facing the garden. Howie's parents were quarrelling loudly.

'They're drunks,' whispered Jeff. 'My dad says they're always drinking.'

'Look,' I said. 'Someone's coming.'

A dark figure walked up to the house. It was Howie, and there was somebody with him—a girl. He kissed her and we glanced at each other, frowning. We saw them step into the living room. Howie ignored his parents, pushing the girl up the stairs. Then his father grabbed his shoulder and Howie turned abruptly, raising a fist. His father let go his grip and Howie disappeared up the stairs.

His parents left the house and walked right past us, still arguing. Then a light was lit in a room on the second floor. At the same moment the loud noise of beating drums and screeching guitars from Howie's stereo echoed around the garden.

'We have to find a better spot,' Roland whispered.

I looked around. There was a shed behind us with a flat roof. I pointed at it and Jeff and Roland nodded their heads. As silently as mice, we crawled across the garden, climbed up onto the shed and then lay down flat on the roof. From here we could see straight into Howie's room. He was sitting on the bed with the girl, kissing her like a madman.

'Yuck.' Jeff gulped. 'This is disgusting.'

I had to cover my mouth to stifle my laughter.

'Well,' Roland whispered in his usual calm way, 'at least he isn't likely to be looking out the window, is he?'

He gave us a sign that he was going to have a look around. Jeff and I nodded and Roland disappeared off the roof.

Jeff and I lay side by side in silence, tense as bowstrings. I wondered if Manny had really called him, like Jeff had told me. Manny always called me. Why on earth should he suddenly call Jeff, especially after what had happened today?

I'd known Jeff since before Manny moved into our part of town, and somehow that made Jeff more of a friend. Yet Manny was really a better friend. With Manny you could talk about anything, or just sit quietly reading or drawing. But with Jeff you always had to be doing something—preferably competing. He could never relax. When I wasn't in the mood for that, Jeff became grumpy and nasty. Manny was never like that. Sometimes

Manny was so serious and thoughtful, like a grown man. It was almost as if he were in pain, deep within, but could never tell anyone his secrets.

I was ripped from my thoughts by Jeff punching me in the shoulder.

'He's signalling to us,' he whispered.

We crawled backwards, climbed silently from the roof and stole, half crouched, to where Roland was waiting.

'Take a look at this,' he said.

In front of us, on the wall, was an iron box, its bent and rusty door ajar. Roland opened the door and inside was a fire hose. Attached to it was a heavy steel nozzle with a trigger to control the water flow.

Jeff looked at Roland with a big question mark on his face.

'What are you going to do with this?'

Roland started to roll out the hose as silently as he could.

'You two find a ladder somewhere,' he whispered.

'But why?' Jeff insisted. 'What's the plan?'

'Just do it,' Roland hissed.

My heart was beating fast as I looked around, sneaked over fences, peeked into sheds in the gardens, hoping no one would notice us. The night air was crackling with electric tension. Finally, I found an old ladder. I signalled to Jeff and we carried it to Roland.

'What now?' Jeff whispered, sweating in excitement.

Roland whispered his plan hurriedly and Jeff and I were dumbstruck for a second. But there was no time to waste. We had to do it. Now.

The loud music poured out of Howie's window as we raised the ladder underneath it. From his post, Roland raised his thumb and started turning a handle in the iron box. Jeff supported the ladder while I climbed up slowly, my legs trembling, holding the steel nozzle in my right hand.

I approached the window slowly, rung by rung. What if Howie suddenly looked out?

When I had almost reached the top of the ladder, I was high enough to peer inside, and I prepared for the worst.

Howie was still on his bed with the girl wrapped around him, kissing away in oblivious bliss, completely unaware that the terrible Revenge of the Red Dragon was about to hit him hard.

I stood stock still on the top rung, trying not to tremble, which was difficult. I could feel the cold pulsing of the water pressure in the hose, and my fingers were frozen stiff. I had to use all my strength just to keep the hose still in my hands.

I stuck my hand under the window and shoved with all my might. The window flew up and the music blared in my face, vocals screaming.

In a flash I placed the nozzle on the windowsill, aiming right at the spot where the lovers' lips met. Then I shouted out at the top of my voice, 'For Socrates!' I cocked back the trigger on the nozzle, and the hose jumped and squiggled as the ice-cold water shot straight across the room, hitting the romantic couple hard in the face.

What happened next must have taken just a couple of seconds, but to me it was like a movie scene in slow motion. Howie and the girl were thrown back against the wall from the force of the blast, like rag dolls with hands and feet spread helplessly in thin air. Howie tried to leap to his feet, but I kept aiming at his face, so it was impossible for him to stand up. The girl just curled up in the corner, screaming with terror, while the water attacked Howie, pounding him and kicking the feet out from under him, so he fell to the floor.

My fingers were paralysed with cold and I was beginning to lose control of the hose as it jerked back and forth like a living thing in my hands. Posters of rock 'n' roll bands were washed off the walls, books were flushed off the shelves and finally the stereo was drowned and electric sparks flew into the air.

Suddenly the hose tore itself from me and

I lost my balance, almost falling from the ladder. I climbed down as fast as I could, while the hose slid further into the room, like an evil snake slithering towards its victim. I fell on the soft grass and Roland grabbed me by the collar and dragged me away. We ran over to the shed and climbed up onto the roof with lightning speed.

From there we could see straight into the bedroom. Howie was chasing the hose, trying desperately to grab the nozzle and turn off the water. The hose finally took one decisive lunge and bucked through the window, shattering the glass. It sailed out into the garden, where it lay hissing and twisting, and gushing water in every direction.

Howie appeared at the window, shivering, teeth clattering and trembling with rage.

'You'll pay for this, you bastards!' he cried.

Roland stood up on the roof, raising his fist against him.

'There's no need for that! You've earned it! Bastard!'

Jeff and I jumped to our feet, shouting at the top of our lungs.

'For Grandma Dell! For Socrates!'

Then we climbed off the roof, laughing ourselves delirious, running away to safer territory.

'That was sensational!' Jeff cried.

'Talk about a wet kiss!' Roland said, chuckling.

'When you yelled through the window,' Jeff said to me, 'I laughed so hard I almost whizzed in my pants!'

'Well, why didn't you? No one would have noticed.' Roland grinned. 'Not with all that water running!'

10

THE STORY of the Great Avengers of Socrates spread like wildfire through the neighbourhood. And suddenly nobody was really afraid of Howie anymore. The threat he'd always represented had simply evaporated, like rain on a hot summer's day. The little kids called him names if they saw him— Howie the Hose, Shower-Howie. If he tried to chase them they just split up and ran in all directions, shrieking with laughter. At last it had been shown that he wasn't invincible. He'd had to bow to a greater opponent: the Order of the Red Dragon.

He stopped skulking around the Ground

in the evenings, but sometimes he would appear on his motorcycle, flexing his muscles by revving his engine and spraying the gravel in front of Grandma Dell's house, just for the satisfaction of seeing her come to the door, cross and frowning. Apart from those rare occasions, he virtually disappeared. We were the heroes of the day.

We started practicing fencing every afternoon on the field next to the Ground, and usually there was a small crowd of onlookers. Each morning we held a meeting at Roland's Round Table, deciding our Code of Behavior, reading Roland's exciting books on knighthood and discussing whom we could help in our part of town. There were many elderly men and women who needed someone to shop for groceries, run errands for them or walk the dog.

About a week after the Great Revenge, Manny and I went downtown to buy a new plug fuse for Grandma Dell's oven. The two of us hadn't been alone together for some time, and I could feel that he needed to talk. Jeff was still bullying him now and then. He always said he was just joking, but it was like he couldn't hold back sometimes, and Manny, being the youngest, was the easiest prey.

'I know you and Jeff are good friends,' Manny said. 'But it's no fun to get pounded on just because you're youngest. He would never dare to do that to you or Roland.'

'I know,' I said, searching for something to say that would make him feel better. 'But now we're in the Order, we're all equal.'

'Jeff doesn't seem to see it that way,' Manny said.

'He will,' I said with conviction. 'I will make him understand.'

Manny looked at me and smiled.

We got the fuse and took it to Grandma Dell, but her fuse box was a mess. There was no way I could work out where to put the fuse, and we were running late for a meeting at Roland's place.

'Don't worry,' Grandma Dell said. 'I'll ask my nephew to mend this, if he ever shows up. Run along, boys.'

When we arrived at Roland's, he and Jeff were in a hot debate about something.

'Finally,' Roland said when we came in. 'Now we can start the meeting.'

Jeff was all red in the face and Roland had an angry look.

'Well then, Jeff,' said Roland. 'Your proposal. We're all listening.'

Jeff was uneasy in his seat, but I knew the stubborn glint in his eyes all too well. Then he grinned, as if he was sure that I, at least, would look favourably on his proposal.

'I was just saying that now is the time to go to war.'

Manny and I stared at him in blank astonishment.

'With whom?' I asked.

'Anyone!' Jeff said, smiling. 'I mean, there are lots of boys from the big estate, going about in groups and fighting.'

'But that's far away,' Manny said, 'and they haven't done anything to us.'

'I know that,' Jeff answered harshly. 'But we could show them that we're the best.'

There it was. Best. And I'd begun to think that Jeff had knocked off the competition bit. If anything, his ambitions had just grown bigger.

'Best at what?' Manny asked.

'At fencing, of course! And fighting!'

He could see that we didn't think it was a very brilliant idea.

'But we fence almost every day,' I said. 'Why bother to start a fight with someone just to show them how good we are at it? I mean, they might be better, for all we know!'

'I was just saying that it would liven things up a bit,' Jeff said defensively. 'Fighting someone rather than just practicing all the time.'

He was getting really angry.

'It would be very different if someone attacked you or some of us,' I said. 'Then we'd fight, of course. But not just for nothing.'

'I didn't mean just for nothing!' Jeff blustered. 'I meant a challenge, a duel, a competition.'

'That's of course something else altogether,' Roland said. 'That's not the same thing as war.'

'Well that's what I meant,' Jeff said angrily.

All the same, I knew he had meant war.

'Let's take a vote,' Roland said. 'Who is in favour of holding a fencing competition, inviting whomsoever wishes to challenge us?'

Jeff raised his hand and glanced around the table. Roland, Manny and I didn't move. Jeff glared at us and lowered his hand.

'Then I don't want to be a member of this childish club anymore,' he announced, standing up and looking me straight in the eyes. 'You guys can keep on fencing for a bunch of nursery-school kids; I've had enough of it. You can pretend you're knights, for all I care. Who's ever heard of knights who never went to war?'

'There was generally a reason for that,' Roland said calmly.

'I couldn't care less what you say,' Jeff

shouted. 'You think you're so smart. You think you know so much because you have an ancient family. You think you're something special just because of that?'

'Who are you to attack him?' I shouted, standing up so abruptly that my chair fell to the floor. 'It's *you* that thinks you're special. And you're constantly picking on Manny, just because he's younger than you. You're no better than Howie!'

'You talk so much rubbish!' Jeff growled.

'You're an idiot!' I shot back at him.

'And you're a coward!' he cried.

'Then get out and try to find someone else to tolerate you!' I shouted in fury. 'You and your goddamn arrogance!'

Jeff stomped out of the room and slammed the door behind him. I stood still, trembling with rage. We were silent for a long time. Finally I picked up my chair and sat down. Roland and Manny looked at me as if they were waiting for me to say something, but I had nothing to say.

'Maybe he will be calmer tomorrow,'

Roland said. 'His anger will subside, no doubt.'

'No, it won't,' I whispered.

'I'm sure he didn't mean what he said,' Roland added. 'He was just angry. People say stupid things when they're angry.'

'He meant every word,' I said. 'I know. He's like that.'

We sat in silence for a while. Then Manny sighed and I could hear that he was relieved.

'Well, maybe this was for the best,' he said.

'Yes. Maybe,' Roland said thoughtfully.

The Eagle runs up the street with a lump in his throat. *They don't understand me*, he thinks. *They never understand anything, the stupid fools.* He runs up the stairs, straight into his bedroom, and throws himself on the bed. He buries his face in the soft pillow. *Why did you have to shout at me, Benjamin? Why did you get all riled up against me? Why did you make me so angry? I didn't want to be angry. I didn't want to say those words. Why couldn't you be on my side? Why couldn't you just be my friend? Benjamin, why couldn't you?*

Three days went by and I didn't run into Jeff in our block of flats or outside either. It was as though the earth had swallowed him whole. However, I was not going to check on him or talk to him. It was he who started it; he could come and find me. Anyway, he owed Roland and me an apology. And I was not going to turn the other cheek this time. It was his turn to be humble. I just stopped thinking about him. For all I knew he'd probably gone with his parents to their summer cottage in the country. Maybe everything would be back to normal when he came back. Yes. Maybe.

11

AGAIN AND AGAIN I was just about to doze off, when I jolted wide awake. Who was whispering my name so loud that I couldn't fall asleep? Or was it just my imagination? I tried to lie still and stared at the wall above my bed.

Peculiar shadows were dancing on the wall; red and yellow wisps swayed back and forth, all the way up to the ceiling. I was half asleep and yet awake. It seemed as though my dream wasn't waiting for me to fall asleep, but had decided to start without me.

As I stared at the kaleidoscope on the wall, it gradually dawned on me that I wasn't dreaming at all. I sat up in bed and looked around me. The eerie glow came from outside. I stepped out of bed and went over to the window. Grandma Dell's house was in flames. Tongues of fire burst out of the windows and up the walls, stretching red and angry into the purple sky. The greedy flames devoured the leaves, turning the trees into giants' torches, illuminating the night.

I was screaming at the top of my lungs when my parents rushed in. My father ran to call the fire department and my mother took me in her arms. I tore myself free and banged my fists against the window. I couldn't look away.

Lights came on in the neighbouring houses and people appeared on their balconies, clumsy in their terrified silence. Why didn't anyone do something? Grandma Dell was doomed.

Someone was moving over the Ground, a shadow running in between the swings and past the wooden tower, jumping lightly over the fence and sprinting towards the burning house. It was Howie the Hood.

The son of a bitch, the murderer! Was that monster making sure that Grandma Dell would be burnt to ashes? Was he going to stand guard in case she came out, so he could toss her back in? I was gritting my teeth and weeping in helpless rage.

Howie started to run around the house, shouting something. What the hell was he doing? He stopped outside the front door and the merciless flames roared at him. He zipped up his leather jacket and pulled on his motorcycle gloves. Then he charged into the burning house and disappeared behind the wall of fire.

Time stood still. In the distance sirens wailed, drawing closer and closer. The entire side of the house facing me was engulfed in flames. The house was just a howling blaze. And then the roof caved in and sparks leaped into the air like a million fireflies, swirling in an ominous dance with the blackest of smoke.

Then Howie appeared where the front door of the house had been. He held a bundle in his arms, and his jacket smoked. He staggered a couple of steps away from the fire, and then he stumbled and fell, coughing, to his knees.

The fire engine and ambulance came screaming around the corner and their stark, cold headlamps lit up this weird scene: Howie the Hood, crouched on his knees with Grandma Dell in his arms like a baby, giving her the kiss of life.

I, Benjamin Dove, the Secretary of the Noble Order of the Red Dragon, Defender of the Weak and the Innocent, had done nothing, while Howie the Hood, the villain, the murderer of animals and the tormentor of children, had risked his own life for the sake of an old woman who was probably his archenemy.

12

GRANDMA DELL'S life hung in the balance for several days. But gradually she regained her strength, and after another week she was on her way back to health. Howie, on the other hand, had been severely burned and would most likely have to stay in the hospital for a long time.

Grandma Dell was moved to the rehabilitation ward, where she was to stay until the doctors decided she was fit enough to go back home. But what home? She had no home to go to. The only thing left standing was the concrete foundation of her little house. Everything she owned had been burnt to a cinder.

The investigators found out that the fire had started in the fuse box, so it was really nobody's fault. But I knew that if I'd had a little more time that day, when Manny and I were late for the meeting at Roland's house, I might have worked out which fuse to change and this would probably never have happened.

'You can't blame yourself for that,' Grandma Dell said, smiling and stroking my cheek gently. 'No one can prevent something they don't know is going to happen, can they now?'

Her room overflowed with flowers from everyone in our part of town. Roland, Manny and I sat by her bedside and delivered messages and get-well-soon cards from children and adults alike.

'I always knew I had many wonderful friends,' she said. 'It's awful to have to leave them all.'

'What do you mean, "leave them"?' Roland asked.

'Well, I don't have a home anymore, do I?'

We looked at one another, but couldn't find words to offer her any comfort.

'Then there's that punk, my nephew,' she said, frowning. 'He says he can get me a room in a nursing home, if I allow him to sell the lot to the city.'

'And are you going to do it?' Manny asked.

'Dear child, what else can I do? I'm just an old nobody. I don't have a choice.'

It was so unlike Grandma Dell to talk like that. She'd always been so strong and self-assured. Now she seemed lost and fragile.

On our way out of the hospital, we passed Howie's room. We peered cautiously in through the half-open door. His face was covered with bandages, like a mummy. He lay so perfectly still that he didn't even seem to be breathing.

We closed the door quietly. A nurse came walking down the hall.

'Were you going to visit Howard?' she asked.

'No,' Roland said. 'We just wanted to know if he was all right.'

'Well, maybe he would be if anybody came to visit him. Hasn't he got any friends? And where are his parents? Do you know them?'

We shrugged our shoulders but couldn't answer. She looked at us and heaved an irritated sigh.

'Do try to contact someone from his family. It's as if he doesn't have a soul in the world. I think he feels downright lousy, if you ask me. And somebody should be proud of him. After all, he saved that woman's life.'

Dad and I were cleaning up after supper, washing the plates and looking out the window at Grandma Dell's empty lot.

'Her nephew called me today,' Dad began.

'Oh?' My mother raised an eyebrow. 'What did he want?'

'He wants me to talk to her about the lot.

The city wants it, and he can get her a room in a nursing home.'

'Is that supposed to sort everything out, then?' Mum said.

'I don't think she wants to go there,' I said.

'That's exactly what her nephew said,' Dad concurred.

'And he wants you to help him change her mind, does he?' Mum asked.

'I think so,' Dad answered, looking a little uncomfortable.

'What a loving nephew he is,' Mum said, frowning. 'That man has a house big enough to take her in.'

'Would you come with me tomorrow, Benjamin, to visit her?' Dad said.

I nodded, half in reverie. It was odd looking out the window since the debris of the house had been cleaned up. No trees, no garden. What in the world would be done with the lot? Perhaps a block of flats would be thrown up, or an ugly car park.

How strange that everything could change so quickly. And there wasn't a thing that anybody could do for Grandma Dell. How unfair.

The next day the sun beamed cheerfully through the hospital window and the sweet aroma of flowers filled the room as Dad tried to explain to Grandma Dell that it wouldn't be that bad going to a nursing home.

'You won't have a care in the world,' he said. 'And I'm sure your nephew will try to get as much for the lot as possible, so no money worries either. Nothing to lose, everything to gain.'

'So what?' she challenged. 'What difference does it make if I get a bed and board but lose all the friends I have? You call that nothing?'

'We'll all come to visit, and you'll come to visit us!' My dad tried to soothe her.

'Well it's not the same,' she retorted stubbornly.

'Oh, you'll get used to it in no time,' said Dad.

Grandma Dell shot him an angry look.

'I've lived in that house since I moved to the city, forty years ago. I raised my sons there, and I lost them all, but I still had my home. I worked hard to keep it, I took in washing, I sewed clothes for women all over town. I did anything and everything just to keep my home. I've watched the children in the neighbourhood grow up and have families of their own, like you, Stephen. Do you remember when you were a small boy and came running to me when someone had pushed you over?'

Dad nodded and studied his fingernails. Grandma Dell continued.

'I've lived in this place for too long to go off and get used to new people, new houses. That place is my home—and all of you are my family.'

Her voice trembled with rage and anguish. Then she lay down on the pillow, heaved a harsh sigh and pulled up the covers.

Dad and I were speechless. What could we say?

'I think it's best if you leave now,' she said, and I could hear she was crying.

A lump swelled in my throat and my eyes burned. Why did she have to have such a rough time, this old woman who was kind and helpful to everyone? Why could no one help her?

In the quiet of a half-lit hospital room, a young man lies still, listening to the silence. His head is wrapped in fresh bandages; only his mouth and one eye are visible. The eye is wide open, staring into the semidarkness. Nobody has come to see him. His parents have gone; he is sure of that. Sometimes they're gone for days, weeks even. They're bound to be holed up somewhere, drinking. They probably don't even know that he's in hospital. The doctor and the nurses try to be nice to him, asking him questions about his parents, but he doesn't answer. Doesn't want to talk to anyone. Just wants to be left in peace.

He saved her life, and it feels good. It was

good that he was close by, good that she didn't die. She would have if he hadn't busted into that hellfire and hustled her out of there. It was good that he was the one who saved her. She's always so good to everyone.

*Think she'd be good to me?* he asks himself.

13

THE THREE OF US sat on the swings at the Ground, occasionally glancing through the fence at the foundations where Grandma Dell's house used to be. I had told Roland and Manny about my visit to her that afternoon, and now we sat mute and pondering.

Roland stood up, picked up a pebble, threw it in the air and let it fall into the palm of his hand.

'If only there were something we could do,' he said, squeezing the stone in his fist.

'What?' Manny sighed.

'I don't know,' Roland said. 'But the way I

see it, this is a true challenge for the Order.'

Manny gave him a confused look.

'You're saying we should pick up our swords and fight her nephew?'

'No.' Roland laughed. 'This situation calls for a different kind of fight.'

'I have no ideas,' Manny said, with a shrug.

'What if . . . ,' Roland began, and then paused for a moment. 'What if we took up a collection for her, you know, clothes, furniture, even . . . '

'Money!' Manny said suddenly and jerked up on the swing.

'Money?' I said, and looked at Roland.

He was waiting for the pebble to fall in his open palm. He caught it and clenched his fist around it, looking at us with a big smile. In a flash the same thought shot through our minds, like a million lightbulbs being switched on at the same time. Our eyes burning with excitement, the words blurted out of our mouths:

'To build a house!'

'A new house!'

'Loads of money!'

'Loads and loads!'

We leapt to our feet, talking faster than we could form the words, almost shouting at each other in excitement.

'We'll go to everybody in the neighbour-hood!'

'Yeah, and the streets beyond too!'

'And we could sell something too! Like, I don't know . . . '

'Like biscuits!'

'And fish for cat food!'

'And collect bottles and cans!'

'We'll get all the kids to help us go door-to-door!'

'And save up tons of money!'

'And put it all in the bank!'

'Heaps of money!'

Suddenly the problem was solved. It was so easy, almost too easy, now we knew what to do. We ran across the Ground, jumped over the fence and walked around the old foundations. We could almost see the new house rise up, right before our eyes.

'We have to collect money to buy timber and nails, and tiles on the roof . . . '

'And we have to get carpenters . . . '

'And buy paint . . . '

'And windows . . . '

'And glass . . . '

'Kitchen sink . . . '

'Bathtub . . . '

'And all the pipes . . . '

'And doors, don't forget doors . . . '

'Maybe it's impossible,' I said, and sat down, deflated. 'It all costs so much. I mean —a whole house! It will take years!'

'Yes, but if we just begin,' Roland encouraged me. 'If we only start this thing, who knows what will come our way! Of course we'll succeed. We must! We will, that's all!'

We bounced the idea back and forth while the sun moved slowly over the clear sky. We felt we had already begun Operation Resurrection, walking around the foundations, imagining the new house and how much we'd need of this and that.

We were so busy talking that we didn't notice Jeff until he was standing right next to us.

We fell silent instantly, glancing at each other and then at him. I felt awkward and angry at the same time; I didn't want him around anymore.

'Hi,' he said in a low voice.

'Hello,' Roland said gently.

'Are you going to collect money for Grandma Dell?' Jeff said, and I could hear excitement in his voice.

'Maybe,' Roland answered.

'Have you been eavesdropping?' I said.

'I was just walking past,' he muttered. 'I can't help if I overheard what you were saying.'

'You know that all matters discussed in the Order are strictly confidential,' I said harshly.

Jeff bowed his head. I got the feeling that he was just acting humble, making us believe that he was really sorry. But I wanted him to say it out loud.

'Anyway,' he said finally, 'I was on my way to see you.'

'We thought you'd resigned from the Order,' Roland reminded him.

'Yeah, slamming the door behind you,' I chimed in.

Jeff said nothing for a while, just stood there studying the ground in front of him.

'I just wanted to talk to you guys a little, that's all,' he said, so low I could barely hear him.

'About what?' I said.

'About whether I could join up again,' he said, without looking up.

The three of us exchanged glances; we were all thinking the same thing. We were glad to be rid of him. He'd beaten Manny in anger and then pretended it was nothing. He was arrogant and bossy and his constant competing ruined every game.

'All those in favour of reinstating Jeff into

the Order, raise their hands,' Roland said dryly. No one moved a muscle.

Jeff bowed his head, turned around and shuffled slowly away, then burst into a furious run and disappeared into the block of flats.

I felt lousy; I was sorry for him and ashamed of myself. After all, he had been my friend. It shouldn't have had to happen this way, but I reminded myself that it was his own doing. We stood silent and motionless for a while. Then we arranged a new meeting, said good-bye to each other and went home.

He rushes up the stairs, the tears burning his eyes. *Why have you turned against me? What have I done to deserve this?* As he comes in, his father yells something from the living room, demanding to know where he's been. He can yell all he wants; for once the boy couldn't care less. His own anger burns inside him, the flames roaring in his ears. He storms into his bedroom, not hearing the shouting, his mother, his father, the banging on the door. He buries his face in the pillow, clenches his fist and bashes the wall, the bed, the pillow, harder, harder. He is lonely and afraid. He hasn't got any friends anymore. And he can't understand why.

14

THE FOLLOWING DAYS were busy
ones for the Knights of the Red Dragon. We
went door-to-door, dressed in full regalia, collecting money in our helmets. At first we
went together, but we quickly saw that it
made better sense to split up and divide the
territory among the three of us. We rang
doorbells, introduced ourselves and explained
the mission. Everyone gave money, some quite
a lot, and no one refused to donate something.

When my helmet was full of pennies and
banknotes, I ran back to Roland's house. He
had a wooden chest in his room, which we

intended to fill before taking it to the bank.

After three days of collecting, the chest was almost overflowing, so we carried it between us down the street, through our part of town and into the bank.

We walked straight up to the cashier, with the wooden chest between us. She looked up, maybe a little amazed to see such a decorative battalion stride in and plonk a chest in front of her.

'Now what have we here?' she asked with a smile. 'Pirate treasure?'

'We'd like to open an account,' Roland answered, in the clear, precise tone he generally adopted when he spoke to adults.

The staff looked up from their work. Some of the customers were giggling. Then a tall bald man in a striped suit came dashing out of an office from behind the counter, obviously in a hurry. When he saw us, he stopped in his tracks. A big smile formed on his face.

'Whose castle have you been robbing?' he asked, and the staff laughed.

'Go on now, boys,' the cashier said. 'Just play outside, will you?'

'Maybe it's an armed robbery, eh? Watch out, folks!' the bald man cried, and everybody laughed.

Then Roland unlocked the chest and opened it. The laughter died down when they saw the pile of money inside.

'As you can see, we need to open an account,' Roland said.

'Where did you get all this money, boys?' the bald man asked, with a serious look.

'We have taken up a collection for an old lady who lost her house and all her possessions in a fire over in our neighbourhood last week,' answered Roland. 'Of course, you're all very welcome to contribute,' he added with a smile. 'But first we'd like to deposit this, if you'd be so kind.'

The cashier gave the bald man a questioning look. He nodded at her, smiling.

'And in whose name will the account be?' asked the cashier, looking at each of us in turn.

'The Order of the Red Dragon,' answered Roland in a clear voice.

The other cashiers smiled at each other, looking as if they were very pleased with their new customer.

'Well, I'll be!' sighed the bald man, and gave the cashier a wink. 'Are you by any chance recruiting new members?'

'Perhaps,' Roland said. 'It all depends on how much you're willing to contribute to the cause. If you show you have a noble heart, then we'll be glad to take you on. But,' he added, smiling and raising a finger, 'membership of the Order of the Red Dragon doesn't come cheap.'

Everybody laughed, the bald man most of all.

'You're a quick one, aren't you, son?' he said, looking at his watch, heading for the door. 'Susan!' he called to the cashier, who was counting the contents of the chest. 'When you've finished counting, double the amount, as a contribution from the bank. No, triple it! And make sure these gentlemen are booked for a meeting with me, first thing in the morning!'

Then he hurried out the door. The cashiers glanced at one another, shaking their heads and smiling.

'Who was that?' Manny asked.

'That was the manager,' said our cashier, Susan. 'And if I know him, he will most certainly want to be inducted formally into your Order.'

'Well, he most certainly has earned it!' Roland said.

Susan finished counting, opened the account and tripled the amount, all while we sat there, speechless, in front of her. Finally she handed us a receipt, smiling. We inspected it carefully and drew our breath.

'Until tomorrow morning, then,' Susan said. 'You're booked for a meeting with Mr. Grant at nine o'clock.'

We walked on clouds all the way back home, Roland clutching the receipt for the full amount of the day's deposit.

'I told you something would come our way,' he said proudly. 'But now we just have to keep up the good work. There's no time to waste!'

'For Grandma Dell!' we shouted. Then we ran, each in his own direction, to raise more funds.


The boy is standing in an alley in an unfamiliar neighbourhood. He slipped in there, just in time, before Benjamin could see him. *There he runs*, the boy is thinking. *Running with his helmet full of money, collecting for Grandma Dell. I wish I was running with him; I bet I could collect more than any of them. But they threw me out. They don't want me with them, so I don't care anymore. I have new friends. Better friends. And before too long, the Order of the Red Dragon will suffer. They all will. Benjamin will. I wish none of this had happened. But it has. It wasn't my fault, and there is nothing I can do about it.*

He watches as his former friend disappears into the doorway of a big block of flats. Then he steals out of the alley and runs down the street, to a secret meeting with his new friends.

15

MR. JACOB GRANT, the bank manager, opened his office with a smile and offered us a seat on a soft leather coach. He sat at his desk, looking at each of us in turn, and said: 'It is not often one runs into boys like you. It happens far too seldom, as a matter of fact. It's easy to believe that all kids nowadays are just a bunch of vandals, but you're proof of the opposite. I know I was no angel when I was your age, that's for sure. And look at me now!' He gave a big grin and flung his arms out. 'But tell me about this lady who lost her house.'

We told him the whole story, about everything Grandma Dell had done for us and other kids in our part of town, and for every-body. We told him about Socrates and Howie, and that it was indeed Howie who had rescued her life. Then I told him what Grandma Dell had said to me and Dad: that she would rather die than lose her adopted family in our part of town.

'And you want to raise enough money to build her a new house? Is that it?' he asked.

'Exactly,' Roland answered. 'At least we're going to do what we can. We have to do something.'

Mr. Grant leaned back in his chair and looked at us for a moment, pressing the fin-gertips of each hand together.

'A new house costs a lot of money,' he pointed out, 'even though it's just a small wooden house. Do you really think you can do it?'

'If we don't give up,' Roland answered, 'I'm sure we can. We've decided to stand together and do everything in our power to help her.'

'If we don't do it, nobody else will,' Manny added. 'Even her own nephew is trying to get her lot away from her and sell it . . . '

' . . . and it's just so unfair,' I finished.

Mr. Grant smiled.

'And you are true knights,' he said, 'who battle against injustice in the world, right?'

'That is our mission,' Roland said, and Manny and I nodded.

'Well then,' Mr. Grant continued, 'tomorrow I'm attending a meeting with the Board of Directors. I'm going to tell them about you and your noble mission. I cannot promise you anything, but I know they will listen to my suggestions. And of course,' he added, 'it would help if they knew they were not just dealing with a mere bank manager, but a true Knight of the Order.'

'Then you'll have to choose an insignia,' Roland said, smiling.

'Ah yes,' Mr. Grant said, thinking for a moment. 'When I was a boy we used to play cowboys and Indians, and I always wanted to be an Indian called Little Wolf. Isn't that a good one? A wolf?'

'Great!' Manny approved.

'That's perfect,' I said.

'Then that's taken care of,' Mr. Grant said. 'And now I think we should adjourn to the outer office. I wouldn't want my employees to miss the ceremony.'

We followed him out to the main area and Mr. Grant addressed his employees.

'Your attention please. A very special ceremony is about to take place, and I would like you, the employees of this establishment, to serve as my witnesses.'

The staff gathered around us, smiling and whispering, looking curiously at our costumes and weapons.

Mr. Grant went down on bended knee before Roland and bowed his head. The morning sun shone through the blinds and made a striped pattern on his polished, bald dome.

Roland unsheathed his sword and laid the

sword tip on Mr. Grant's left shoulder, saying in a solemn voice:

'For justice!'

Then he moved the sword tip to Mr. Grant's right shoulder.

'Against injustice!'

Then he touched Mr. Grant's bald head lightly with the sword tip.

'I dub thee Knight of the Order of the Red Dragon.'

Then he raised his sword in the air and proclaimed in a clear voice:

'Sir Jacob the Wolf, stand and be recognised.'

Mr. Grant stood up, smiling broadly, and bowed to Roland.

'I am honoured, Sir Roland,' he said in a low voice.

The employees cheered, clapped their hands and whistled. Mr. Grant turned a laughing face to them and made a deep bow.

The three of us were all smiles as we looked at one another. Having a bank manager in the Order was definitely not a bad move, especially since the goal of our mission was to raise money!

We shook hands with a very happy Sir Jacob Wolf, and the staff applauded as we departed. We'd truly had the most unbelievable morning in our lives.

We arrived at Roland's house for a late breakfast, telling his mother excitedly about everything. Then we hurried out again to collect more money, leaving Roland's mother looking completely bewildered.

It was late afternoon when I finally came to the last entrance in one of the block of flats to the north of our part of town. It was not a very nice neighbourhood and I hadn't collected as much as I had hoped for. Still, I was determined to finish this last entrance. It was time consuming to cover the whole building, because each entrance had five floors, and each floor had three flats. I decided to start at the top, as usual, and work my way down the staircase.

Nobody answered the door on the top

floor, nor the next floor below. On the third floor I rang a doorbell, almost sure that nobody would answer. Then the door opened just a little, and the face of Eddie the Turd appeared in the crack. He looked at my clothes and grinned.

'What do you want?'

I explained myself and asked for a donation, but he just smirked. From inside the apartment I could smell paint and hear the scratching of sandpaper. Eddie just stood there, saying nothing. I was about to leave when he said, 'Wait here.' Then he shut the door in my face. I waited, but an uneasy feeling in my stomach was telling me to go.

Suddenly the door opened, yawning wide, and I was staring at a horrible black mask, shaped like a bird's head, with a threatening beak. Attached to it was a black-clothed knight, with a shield, a sword and a spear at his side. Behind him stood three more, all dressed in black, with black bird-mask helmets. I started backwards in spite of myself.

'Benjamin Dove of the Order of the Red

Dragon?' thundered the black knight in front, and handed me a roll of paper.

'Give this to your leader, from the Order of the Black Feather.'

They banged their swords into their shields and yelled in one ominous chorus: 'Black Feather! Black Feather!'

And the door slammed shut.

I took off down the stairs as fast as I could, and out onto the street. What was this all about? I buried the letter in my pocket. What if I just threw it away? I didn't even want to read it, because the uneasy feeling in my stomach wouldn't go away.

When I rushed into Roland's room I was surprised to see my father there, sitting next to Roland's father at the Round Table with Roland and Manny.

'Dad,' I said, panting. 'What are you doing here?'

'We've been discussing this fundraising project of yours,' Dad said.

'And frankly, we're a little worried about

it,' Mr. McIntosh added, and the two men exchanged a smile.

'What is there to worry about?' I said, and sat at the table. Roland and Manny looked quite at ease, so I assumed that they knew what was going on.

'Well, we're mainly concerned about what is to become of all this money,' Dad explained.

'In other words,' Roland's father continued, 'we'd like to help you with the work.'

'To build the house,' Dad said.

'But, Dad,' I said. 'You're not a carpenter.'

'I do happen to recognise the business end of a hammer, Benjamin,' Dad said with a laugh.

'What we'd like to do,' Mr. McIntosh continued, 'is talk to other men in the neighbourhood and put a team together.'

'Talk to electricians, plumbers and carpenters, for example,' Dad said. You can't assume that everyone is willing to give his work, even though it's for a good cause. So we'd like to recruit as many volunteers as possible.'

'How much have you saved, so far?' Mr. McIntosh asked.

Roland showed them the deposit slip from the bank. Dad and Mr. McIntosh glanced at it, then at each other, with raised eyebrows.

'I'd think we could at least buy some timber for that amount,' Mr. McIntosh said.

'Certainly,' Dad agreed. 'And if we are going to have the house ready before Grandma Dell is discharged from the hospital, then we'd better roll up our sleeves and get to work.'

They had obviously thought everything out a lot more thoroughly than we had.


And now things began to move. It was as if our collection had started a fever in our part of town; everybody our fathers talked to was eager to do his bit. And those who couldn't give practical help were more than willing to give Grandma Dell something—clothes, kitchenware or even furniture.

Roland's mother came up with the idea of having a cake auction. She called all the mothers in our part of town, and the whole lot of them began baking as though their lives depended on it.

Three days later, a huge pile of pale, fragrant lumber was deposited next to the foundations of Grandma Dell's house. Our fathers, with five other men from our part of town, started to work on the foundation, preparing it for the first phase of the building process. It was then that we knew our dream really would come true.

16

IN THE DARKNESS of a hospital room, an old woman is sitting still on her bed, staring out into the night. It's been a while since she has been so idle. And these lonely days have made her think back on her life, about her late husband and her sons, whom she lost. *What has life given me that it hasn't taken away again?* she thinks. *What do I have left? Why didn't you just let me die, God; burn me up along with every last thing I owned?* But God doesn't answer. There's just the warm breeze breathing lightly through the curtains by the window. And listening to the soft breath of the breeze, a thought comes to her that brings a tiny smile, and a welcome relief to her grieving heart. She eases herself out of bed, puts on a white hospital dressing gown and peers out the door of her room. A nighttime hush blankets the corridor; no one is about. She pads silently down the corridor. *That's right*, she thinks; *that's why I didn't die. There's one thing left.*

Finally she finds him, alone in the night, awake like her. The bandages have been taken from his face; his black hair is singed and his skin is mottled. She sits by the bed in the dark quiet of the night.

'You're awake,' she whispers.

The boy nods, but is reluctant to talk. He doesn't look at her, but gazes at the window, where the warm breeze is breathing through the curtains.

'Well, I wanted to see you,' she says quietly. 'And to thank you.'

'What for?' the boy mutters.

'For saving my life,' she says.

'It's nothing,' he mumbles, but his lips are trembling.

He swallows and there are tears in his eyes. There's silence for a long time. Finally he speaks, without looking away from the window, without drying his tears.

'You know,' he whispers, 'I killed your cat.'

The woman places a warm hand on his arm, squeezing gently, reassuringly.

'I know,' she says. 'You took his life, but you gave mine back to me. So, in a way, we could say we're quits.'

The boy moves his head for the first time, with a puzzled look on his face.

'Quits?'

'Oh, yes,' the woman says, smiling. 'I know there's a reason for everything, a reason you had to do what you did. And I don't blame you for that.'

'You don't?' he whispers.

'No. I know what it's like, not to be loved. I know how far one will go, to get the attention one needs.'

The boy turns his head on the pillow, looking away, gazing at the dark window again.

The tears are now running freely down his cheeks. He bites his lip, trying hard not to give in. But her warmth is too much, her kindness too overwhelming. So, he lets go.

Her voice goes on, in a soothing tone, for a long time. She's saying things that no one has ever said to him, things that are good to hear. She understands everything. Before he knows it, he's fallen into a deep sleep.

She smiles a little, and gently strokes his almost hairless head.

*My blessed saviour*, she thinks. *Now I understand, God, why You take from us. It is so we can learn to value what You give us. And now You have put this boy into my life. No matter how things go from here on, I'm grateful, for You have given me plenty.* All night the old woman talks to God, watching the rhythmic rise and fall of the boy's chest as he sleeps. When daylight creeps through the curtains, she pads silently down the corridor to her own room. And she sleeps all morning, with a tiny smile playing on her lips.

17

FOUR BLACK KNIGHTS stand, shuffling restlessly, in the shipyard. Black masks with bird beaks cover their faces. Their shields are flame red, with a crudely painted black feather in the middle; heavy wooden swords dangle from their belts. One of them is armed with a bow and a quiver filled with black arrows.

'They're not coming,' the largest of them says angrily.

'They're chicken shit,' sneers the one with the bow.

'Piss pots,' taunts the third.

The fourth knight is silent. He's tense and wound up, can't stand still. He shuffles over to a fallen oil drum, sits down and takes off his mask.

'Nervous?' the big guy says, chuckling.

'No. No way,' he answers, combing his sweaty hair back with his fingers. 'Just roasting to death in that mask.'

He stares intently at the shipyard's big iron gate. There's no movement. There's no way down to the shipyard, other than through that gate. *Maybe they're waiting outside? But no, they would come in. Benjamin would, at any rate. Why don't they show up?* He wishes it were all over and done with. Wishes passionately that none of this had ever happened.

'How long have we been waiting?' their leader asks.

'Over an hour,' the bowman answers.

'Told you; they're chicken!' the third chimes in.

*How did it come to this?* he asks himself. *I could have been with them, helping to collect for*

*Grandma Dell's house. Everyone is talking about it, what great kids they are. Now they've begun to build the new house, and it's all thanks to them. And I was left out. These guys are not like Benjamin and Manny, and they're certainly not like Roland. Eddie just gives orders, says, 'Shut up while I'm talking' or 'Do what I say or I'll belt you'. He hasn't said it to me yet, but the other guys do everything he says. They're scared of him. Roland was never like that. But it doesn't matter anymore. This is my new Order, these are my new friends.*

'Let's get out of here,' Eddie grumbles.

'Damn!' the archer complains. 'I was really in the mood for a fight!'

'Save it. They'll come next time, wait and see.' Eddie smirks under his black mask. 'Jeff, you carry my shield,' he barks.

Jeff shoulders his leader's shield. The weight of it presses heavily down on him.

Every day we went to the bank with the proceeds of the day's collection, and every time we made a deposit Sir Jacob Wolf told Susan the cashier to triple the amount. He had the Board's approval to support our cause as he saw fit. As word of that spread around, other businesses around town wanted to take part as well. All the craftsmen donated their work and kept the project going day and night.

The cake auction was held the following Sunday in the garden, next to the foundations of Grandma Dell's house. What Roland predicted had actually happened—we had started it and others had followed. We strolled back and forth in the garden and watched the men work on the building.

Hordes of people gathered at the cake auction. The table was several yards long and groaned under the weight of all kinds of cakes, pies and pastry.

'Man, that makes me hungry,' sighed Manny, wide eyed.

'You said it,' I agreed. 'Reminds me of Jeff's birthday . . . ' I stopped short. We hadn't mentioned Jeff since the day he asked to rejoin the Order. Since then I hadn't even run into him in the stairwell.

'Have you seen him?' Roland asked.

'No,' I answered, feeling uncomfortable, and thrust my hands deep into my pockets. Then I found the note.

I'd decided not to tell the others about it at first, and then the days had been so busy that I'd totally forgotten about it and hadn't even read it myself. Now I pulled it out of my pocket and handed it over to Roland.

'What's this?' he asked, and raised an eyebrow.

I told them about the black knights in the apartment house.

'How could you forget to tell us?' Manny asked.

'I didn't at first,' I said. 'At first I didn't want to mention it, because we had so much to do and I didn't want anything to get in the way.'

'They're challenging us to a battle,' Roland said, and showed us the note. Manny read it aloud:

'*The Black Feather challenges the Red Dragon to be in the shipyard at nine on Thursday evening. You're wimps if you don't show. This is a declaration of war. Show up and fight. Long live the Black Feather.*'

At the bottom of the paper was a bad drawing of a black feather and a sword forming a cross.

'When did they give this to you?' Manny asked.

'Days ago, weeks even,' I said vaguely. I didn't really want to tell them exactly how long I'd been walking around with this note in my pocket.

'Well it's clear that we've missed our great battle,' Roland said, laughing. 'If they really want to fight, then they'll just have to send us another Declaration of War.'

'Yeah, maybe they'll send it with a pigeon, or is this supposed to be a feather from a crow?' Manny giggled.

I didn't laugh. The black masks in the hallway of that flat hadn't been particularly friendly. For some reason I was nervous about the whole thing.

Manny looked like he was too, despite his attempt to make jokes about it. We both looked at Roland.

'We don't have to be afraid, you know,' he assured us. 'We don't have to fight if we don't want to. No one can force us to. And if we do decide to fight them, we don't have to worry either. We're bound to be better fencers than they are; we've been practicing for weeks.'

I sighed with relief. What Roland said made perfect sense.

'But Roland,' Manny hesitated, 'what if they outnumber us, and maybe attack us, you know, without warning?'

'That's pure violence,' Roland said. 'If they do that we must fight to defend ourselves. But a war is nonsense, and we won't fight any wars. It's that simple.'

'That's good,' Manny said, and relaxed.

'Of course not,' I said. 'Of course we don't have to fight if we don't want to.'

'Exactly,' Roland said. 'And now, to turn

the conversation to more important things, what do you say we try to pinch a slice of that cake over there?'

We edged over to the table and eyed the incredible variety of appetising baked goods as they disappeared one after another into the arms of the auction guests. My mum caught us spying and motioned for us to come over to her. She presented me with a big chocolate cake, lavishly decorated with strawberries and whipped cream.

'Here boys, divide this among yourselves and stop drooling over the merchandise,' she said with a smile.

We didn't need to be told twice. We grabbed the cake, ran over to the Ground, ripped off our capes and were transformed in a flash from gallant knights into wild, choco-late-hungry pigs of the lowest sort.

'Mmm,' Manny groaned with his mouth full. 'Bags be a baker when I'm big. It must be the sweetest job in the world.'

'Bags having free cakes delivered home

every day, when you're a baker,' Roland laughed, with a chocolate moustache on his face.

'Bags visiting you every day, when Manny has become a baker!' I said, and burst into laughter.

Manny started giggling uncontrollably, his face covered with chocolate and whipped cream. It was hilarious.

'Bags . . . bags,' he gasped. 'Bags visiting Roland with Benjamin when I've become a baker!'

And that one finished us. We doubled over, tears running down our chocolate-stained cheeks. We couldn't stop laughing at that silly cake joke. We could laugh forever, it seemed, and forget everything else.

He is standing by the window, staring out at the garden and over the Ground. He sneaked into the flat so they wouldn't see him. He feels like a traitor, and it's a feeling that burns deep inside his stomach. There they are, eating cake and laughing and laughing. *It's so unfair. I should be there too. But it's too late. Nothing will ever be the way it was. And it's not my fault!*

There's a meeting tonight and there's only one item on the agenda: the destruction of the Order of the Red Dragon. He is supposed to give all the necessary information. He watches his former friends laughing and clowning around on the grass. Everything they're doing is so much fun, so exciting. *It's so unfair.*

18

THE CARPENTERS worked tirelessly. When the skeleton of the house was ready, the beams of the roof were quick to follow. Then the outer timber walls went up and finally the windows were fitted, with sparkling new glass.

Little by little the garden filled with all kinds of appliances. One morning a bathtub arrived, and a toilet and a sink soon after-wards. Someone had torn down an old garage and had brought all the corrugated iron that was whole and un-rusted, and that same evening the iron was firmly on the roof.

Every day people came to watch the carpenters work and to ask if anything was needed. Everyone wanted to take part, and Grandma Dell's family grew bigger every day. The new house began to take shape before our very eyes.

From the far reaches of storage sheds and attics came dusty old furniture that was duly cleaned, aired and polished. A kitchen table and chairs, a coffeepot and dishes, a dresser and an armchair, a floor lamp, a refrigerator —all materialised seemingly out of nowhere, either used, but in perfect condition, or brand new and straight from the shop.

During the last few days before Grandma Dell was due to leave the hospital, the women in the neighbourhood worked constantly, painting walls and kitchen cabinets, laying carpets and hanging curtains. Their husbands worked on the plumbing, the electricity, installing the appliances and painting the new house in the same colour as the old one. The only things missing were the flowers and the trees, but they would come in time, and of course Grandma Dell had to have something to do herself.

For three whole nights the little house was crowded with people, each hand applying finishing touches, so everything could be as cosy as possible when Grandma Dell came back home. By Saturday evening it was ready at last. A little wooden house with two rooms and a kitchen, just like the old one, stood in the evening sunlight, waiting patiently for its owner.

On Sunday at noon, Dad and I went to pick Grandma Dell up from the hospital. The others were preparing a feast in the garden to celebrate her homecoming.

She sat on the hospital bed, fully clothed, staring listlessly into space. Her tired face brightened into a smile when she saw us.

'Ah, there you are, boys. Thank goodness. All this time lying flat on my back in a sickbed was getting on my nerves.'

We walked with her down the corridor,

towards the main entrance of the hospital.

'How's Howie doing?' my father asked.

'Oh, he'll be fine,' she said.

'Should we pay him a visit before we leave?' Dad suggested.

'Well, that's difficult,' she said. 'He's gone.'

'Gone? You mean he's run away?'

'Ah, Stephen, it's no wonder you don't understand. He's had a hard life, that boy.'

'But isn't he still under the doctor's care? Is he in any shape to look after himself?'

'I told the doctors not to bother, and definitely not to get the police to search for him,' Grandma Dell said sternly. 'He's just as able to look after himself now as ever before. Lord knows he's had practice enough. But he'll be back,' she added, with an assured nod. 'He'll be back.'

In the car on the way home, Dad tried to prepare Grandma Dell, at least a little, for the surprise that awaited her.

'We've planned a little celebration in the

garden, Grandma Dell. Just to welcome you home,' he said.

'Oh, for heaven's sake, Stephen, that's utterly unnecessary. There's no reason to make a fuss over me.'

'Now, don't be shocked, Grandma Dell. There'll be a lot of people there. You have many friends, you know.'

'I know, dear. I know,' she said.

'And there's another thing,' Dad continued. 'I've been talking to your nephew. And I think I've managed to reason with him.'

'Don't mention that hypocrite,' she spat out. 'He thinks I'm just a senile old bat, but he's got another think coming. I can sell my lot myself, thanks very much.'

'Yes, but do you really want to do that?' Dad asked.

'I'm not going to sleep under the stars, that's for sure. I may need to stay with you for a night or two, but the last thing I want is to freeload in someone else's home.'

'You wouldn't be freeloading, and you

know it. You can live with us as long as you like, and we'll be delighted to have you.'

At this, Grandma Dell turned and shook a pointed finger at him.

'Now listen here, Stephen my boy, if you're all plotting to somehow coerce me into sponging off you for the rest of my days, then my answer is no thank you. I've never been a burden to anyone since I was old enough to stand on my own two feet, and I'm certainly not going to start now, at my age. Understood?'

Dad burst out laughing.

'No one's going to drag you into their home against your will. That you can count on, I promise you.'

Grandma Dell shot him a suspicious sideways glance. I could tell she was afraid that someone was going to do her a favour she wasn't prepared to accept.


Dad parked the car on the street in front of our house, out of sight of the garden.

'Run ahead of us, would you Benjamin?' he said. 'Tell everyone we're coming.'

He gave me a wink behind Grandma Dell's back.

I jumped out of the car and took off like a shot, around the corner into the garden.

'You don't have to take my arm like that, Stephen,' I heard Grandma Dell say. 'I'm not disabled, you know.'

'Yes, ma'am,' Dad said, laughing.

Around the corner was the biggest crowd I'd ever seen in one place. It was like a national holiday. The fence around the Ground was laden with ribbons, paper streamers and balloons. Long tables stretched across the garden and four grills were laden with fragrant, sizzling hamburgers and hot dogs. A huge banner had been stretched over the garden, bearing the message: 'Welcome home, Grandma Dell!'

The buzzing and chatter of the crowd was so insistent that I had a hard time getting anyone's attention. Then Roland and Manny came to my assistance. We dispersed among the people, calling, 'She's coming, she's coming.'

The crowd quietened down and gathered into two groups, one on each side of the path that led straight to the house. At the end of the path, right in front of the house, stood the reception committee: our parents and Sir Jacob Wolf.

For a moment everything was silent, except the popping of the frying meat and an occasional twitter from a bird overhead.

Then came the crunch of gravel as my father and Grandma Dell rounded the corner, she leaning on his arm despite all her protests. They walked a few more steps, and then Grandma Dell saw everything at once—the smiling crowd, the banner, the ribbons and balloons . . . and the new house, standing so proudly on the foundations of the old one.

She froze like a statue and didn't even blink. It seemed that time stood still for a moment; the sun didn't move in the sky, the birds fell silent in a middle of a tune, the breeze held its breath and the throng of people was completely motionless.

Then someone began clapping, and the stunned moment came to life in an eruption of cheering and applause.

'Welcome home, welcome home!' everyone shouted.

Grandma Dell clung even harder to my father's arm, completely speechless, her eyes brimming over with tears. Dad led her through the cheering crowd towards the house, where Mum hugged her tight.

'Dearest Grandma Dell. Welcome home.'

Grandma Dell glanced around and squeezed my mother's arms as if she was about to faint.

'What have you done?' she finally managed to whisper. 'What is this? How in the world . . . ?'

'This is from all of us,' Mum said. 'It's not a gift, because we know how much you hate surprises.' The people around them laughed. 'We're just repaying you,' she continued, 'for all you have done for us, and for our children. Everyone here has contributed, in one way or the other, towards rebuilding your house, because we know you'd have done the same for each and every one of us.'

Grandma Dell looked her straight in the eye, as if she couldn't quite fathom what she was saying.

Then Sir Jacob Wolf stepped forward and bowed his glistening bald head to Grandma Dell.

'Madam,' he said, as he kissed her trembling hand. 'It is truly an honour and a pleasure to finally meet the woman I've heard so much about. I have the privilege of presenting you with the key to your new house, which my bank has had the tiniest part in financing, but which is thanks mostly to the magnanimous contributions of your friends and neighbours. It is now yours free and clear, with no obligations whatsoever.'

He put the key in her hand and the crowd gave Mr. Grant three cheers. He answered with his broadest smile and then motioned for silence.

'I must add that this house was not built by money alone. Without friendship and unity of purpose, the first nail would never have been driven. But first and foremost this house stands here because of the noble hearts of three young gentlemen.'

The crowd began clapping and shouting 'Red Dragon, Red Dragon', and before we knew it, hands had grabbed us and we were lifted up and borne along the path to Grandma Dell. She hugged each of us again and again, laughing and crying, muttering: 'My darling boys, oh, my boys.'

Finally she turned to my mother and said in a shaky voice, 'Margaret, I think I'd better sit down now.'

Mum led her up the path and into her new house.

Sir Jacob Wolf sat by a table, smiling at everyone, and Roland and I stood by him while Manny went to get our honorary member his surprise for the day: a brand-new wooden sword and a shield with a painting of a wolf howling at the moon.

Manny came back, hiding the sword and the shield under his cape.

'We've got a little something for you,' Roland said, and grinned.

'Oh?' Sir Wolf said. 'Not a real sword, by any chance?'

'And a shield too,' Manny cried and flung back his cape.

'A sword and a shield!' cried Sir Wolf. 'How utterly terrific!'

He took the sword in his hand and marvelled at the wolf on the shield.

'This will hang on the wall behind my desk,' he said, and slashed the air with his sword. 'At last I'm a real knight!'

And then the party began. There were hamburgers and sausages and fizzy drinks and laughter and chattering all over the garden. The carpenters toasted each other and grew merrier by the mouthful. The fragrance of fried meat wafted on the summer breeze as sausages and hamburgers were devoured and sauces and salads scraped from the bottoms of bowls. Old Joe appeared with his accordion; the carpenters began singing and couples started to dance. It was a day nobody would ever forget, not I, nor Roland, nor Manny. And certainly not Grandma Dell.

Later in the evening, with the party still going strong outside, I sneaked into the house to see how Grandma Dell was doing. She was sitting in an easy chair, alone in the room, looking around her as if she still couldn't believe it was all real, as if the fire had just been a bad dream. As if nothing at all had happened.

She didn't notice me standing in the doorway, and I was about to walk towards her. Then suddenly she covered her face in her hands and I heard that she was weeping very softly. All around her were presents and flowers, and on the table was a sugar bowl full of money. I could barely hear the words she whispered into her hands: 'Thank you, thank you.'

I knew these were not tears of sorrow, but

of happiness, of thankfulness. I eased backwards, out of the doorway, very quietly, because I knew she would want to have this moment all to herself. And it felt very good to be able to give her that moment.

# 19

A BOY in a black leather jacket, covered with burn marks, climbs the stairs to a battered old house in a worn-out part of town.

'Home,' he snorts sarcastically to himself. He has no home.

It's as he thought; his parents have taken off without even bothering to let him know or to find out where he'd been. The house is a wreck as usual; there is a broken chair in the living room, and the kitchen full of empty bottles and dirty dishes.

He hurries upstairs to his bedroom and stuffs a few items of clothing into a small duffel bag. No, this place isn't home, and never was. To hell with his parents, he couldn't care less about them. He's going to take off, maybe get a job on a trawler or a farm, or something.

He opens a drawer and an old photograph catches his eye; it's a picture of a boy around five, tense, wary and frightened. He stares at the picture and feels the familiar lump in his throat. But he's not going to cry. Never again. And he's not going to be frightened anymore. He is going away, never to return. He grabs his bag and dashes out to the waiting motorcycle. He's getting out of here, as fast and as far as he possibly can.

At last she is alone. It's very late, and everybody has gone home. She has never in her life hugged so many people or shaken so many hands in one day. She is exhausted, but still she's wide awake. It's just her body that's tired; her spirit is as fresh as though she has just woken up after a long and nourishing sleep.

It's getting darker in the evenings; it's late summer and the breeze is sweet with the fragrance of flowers, trees and raspberry bushes from around the neighbourhood. The night is quiet, except for a buzzing sound in the far distance. A motorcycle, perhaps.

She puts the kettle on and sits down by the kitchen table, listening. The sound approaches. At last she can hear the vehicle turn into the garden, the unmistakable sound of gravel crunching beneath the wheels, and then the motor is shut off. She is at the door and opens it wide before he has even climbed off his bike. The light from the kitchen streams out, illuminating his solemn face.

She invites him in and he perches politely on a chair by the kitchen table and looks around him, half smiling, half puzzled; was there a fire or was it a dream?

She gives him a cup of tea and some biscuits on a plate. Then she sits down, watching him eat and drink for a while in silence.

'My parents have gone,' he says finally, in a low voice.

'What are you going to do?' she asks.

'I'll find something,' he says. 'A job somewhere. I can take care of myself.'

'I don't doubt that for a minute,' she says. 'But where will you stay in the meantime?'

The boy shrugs and sips his tea, looking out the window. There's another silence, broken only by the occasional late-night chirps of birds, bidding each other good night, from nest to nest.

'You're welcome to live here, if you'd like to,' she says.

The boy gazes out the window and doesn't answer.

'You could stay in the living room. You would have it entirely to yourself.'

'I'd have to pay you rent,' he finally mutters, lowering his head, looking at his hands clutching the teacup.

'I won't hear of it,' she says. 'I'm inviting you to stay here as long as it suits you.'

A smile moves over his lips. His face glows with joy. But he just sits speechless for a while, sipping his tea.

'Thank you,' he says at last.

And the old woman smiles.

20

A YOUNG KNIGHT wakes up in the middle of the night. He was having that dream again, hooves galloping soundlessly over the grey earth. It frightens him. He shivers and looks around the dark room. His mother still hasn't gotten back home from the night shift, his little sister is sleeping soundly in the bed beside him.

There, up against the wall, stands his shield with the lovely white unicorn. *Horses are wonderful; they're strong and powerful,* he thinks. *But unicorns are the strongest. Maybe they don't really exist, not anymore, but if they did, they'd be far stronger than ordinary horses. Because they're the Kings of Horses.*

He lies down next to his little sister, her warm breath gently touching his cheek. He smiles and closes his eyes and the dreams come soaring along, snatching him up on a journey through worlds of adventure. He is smiling in his sleep, because in his dream he is riding a big white unicorn, flying through the sky, and he isn't a bit frightened. The unicorn is his friend and he doesn't have to be scared anymore.

I woke up and felt autumn approaching. Through the window I heard the peculiar sound of rustling leaves, when the wind starts to blow from a different direction, catching the lazy leaves by surprise, turning them over, wringing them off the branches, one by one. Dark clouds moved in to block out the sun, and cold rain showers slashed the windows with heavy drops.

There was still the same bustling activity on the Ground in the daytime, but the evenings had grown darker and colder, and everyone went home earlier. We spent more time indoors, usually in Roland's room, reading books or playing games rather than fencing outside. Our swords and shields remained in place on the wall behind the Round Table.

Of course we had our knightly duties to attend to, running errands for our elderly neighbours as usual, all except for Grandma Dell. Now that Howie had moved in, he did most of her errands. It was strange that he, who had been the terror of our part of town for so long, actually showed himself to be a really nice guy. Sometimes, when we dropped in for a visit, we had a good laugh with him, and he never mentioned the terrible revenge we had brought upon him. It seemed so long ago, as if it had happened in another time, in a different world.

I stayed home most of the day, finishing my model ship. Later, Manny and I were going over to Roland's house. His parents were out for the evening, and we had the whole place to ourselves.

I ran across the street through the drizzling rain, and rang the bell. Manny's mother opened the door and told me he'd already left, so I hurried down the street to Roland's house.

'Hi,' he said when he opened the door. 'Where's Manny?'

'Isn't he here?' I said. 'I stopped by to pick him up, but his mum said he'd already left.'

'Well, he hasn't arrived yet. Must be on his way, then.'

We went into the living room and sat down in front of the TV. There was an exciting film starting in an hour or so, which we'd planned to watch together. While Roland went into the kitchen to make popcorn, I found a giant book in the library, with large illustrations of dinosaurs. For a few moments the house was silent.

Suddenly I heard someone shouting, and then hurried footsteps through Roland's garden, right past the living-room window. Another set of footsteps followed, and then a third and a fourth. There seemed to be a whole group out there. I heard a muffled shout, then some struggling and the pounding of running feet.

Roland appeared at the living-room door.

'What was that?' he said.

The doorbell rang repeatedly, furiously. Roland jumped ahead of me and ran to the front door. Outside there was nothing but stillness and darkness; all motion and noise had ceased. Then came a harsh whisper from out of the dark somewhere, growing louder by the second, and then a heavy thud in the wooden front door, right beside me. I jumped to one side and Roland to the other, staring at the door.

A black arrow had buried its sharp steel tip deep in the door. I grabbed it and pulled it free. A piece of paper was wound around the middle of the shaft. Roland tore it off, read it and then crumpled it in his fist.

'What does it say?' I cried.

'Read it for yourself,' he shouted back, thrusting the piece of paper into my hand and storming back into the house.

I unfolded it and read:

*We have got Manny the Wimp. If you want to rescue him you have to fight. If you think you rule, you must prove it. He will be our prisoner until you show up and fight to set him free. The Black Feather awaits your arrival in the ship-yard tonight. If you dare.*

I rushed into the house, shouting for Roland. He was walking in circles on the living-room floor, hitting furniture with his clenched fist, cursing like a madman, stamping his foot. It was the first time I'd ever heard him swear.

'Roland,' I cried. 'What should we do?'

'We'll go and beat the hell out of those pigs! I swear to you!'

I'd never seen him in this state; I had not even imagined he had it in him. He kept on pacing and swearing.

'Roland, please, stop it. We need a plan!'

'I know! I'm thinking!' he cried. 'We need to get hold of some spears or clubs or something.'

'Clubs? What for? Why clubs?'

'Because these bastards are obviously maniacs,' Roland said, snatching the arrow from my hand. 'I mean, take a look at this!' He pushed the steel tip of the arrow right up to my nose. 'You could kill someone with one of these! Look!'

He was right. The tip was razor sharp.

'Yeah,' I sighed. 'We'd better be ready for anything.'

Roland stood still for a moment, lost in thought. Then he raced through the kitchen, opened the door to the cellar and ran down the stairs. I heard him rummaging through boxes. When he came back he held a broomstick and a steel sword in an ornate scabbard. His eyes were burning.

'Roland, that's a real sword!'

'It certainly is. Aren't they using real arrows?'

'Yes, but . . . you're not really going to use it, are you?'

'If I have to, Benjamin, I will,' he said, and ground his teeth. 'I'm hoping it will scare them stiff, so they'll stop and let Manny go.'

Roland was completely unlike his normal self. He was trembling with a terrible rage.

'Roland, relax,' I said. 'We'll set him free, don't worry.'

He turned to me quickly, his eyes shooting sparks of fire.

'Listen, Benjamin, those guys are maniacs and they've got our Manny; they've kidnapped him, and—I don't know, I just feel it in my bones. They must be crazy; Manny's only nine years old, for heaven's sake. And I bet you anything that these guys are no kids. See, I'm the oldest of the three of us, Benjamin, and . . . well, if anything happens to him, then I'll blame myself.'

'How can you say that, Roland? That's crazy.'

'It's just the way I feel, that's all. Once in

Scotland some guys beat the hell out of me, just to show their strength. Imagine—three against one—some strength, huh? And something tells me these Black Feather lunatics are exactly the same. Guys who are just playing around and having a good time don't make arrows that can kill. They don't kidnap people, either. These guys are nuts, you hear me? Bastard maniacs!'

'Okay. We'll take the sword, then.'

'Unfortunately there's only one,' he sighed.

'That's all right.' I grinned. 'I've got the nasty broomstick.'

The huge trawlers in the shipyard stand motionless, side by side, and seem to scrape the dark sky like colossal sea monsters stranded on a bleak shore. The cold wind howls around steel cables and through rusty iron pipes. A huge fire in the middle of the shipyard casts a ghostly light on four black-clad knights who stand still, staring into the flames. In the flickering firelight, their grotesque bird masks seem to be alive, beaks smirking; eyes squinting, blinking, shifting. Their black capes ripple in the wind like ravens' wings.

The masks give them confidence, anonymity; they're tough and terrifying. Only one of them feels as though he's suffocating beneath his bird-head helmet.

'Jeff, what's the time?' the leader thunders in the silence.

'Eight thirty,' Jeff mumbles from under his mask.

'Watch the gate,' Eddie orders the archer, who runs up to the gate, climbs it and hides in a shadow.

Eddie is confident that it will be an easy battle, Jeff knows. Jeff's told him that Roland is all mouth and won't fight in anger, and that Benjamin is strong but likely to give in to a ruthless attack. Eddie laughed at this. But he hasn't told Jeff where they've hidden Manny. They don't trust him yet.

He's cold and moves closer to the fire. He grabs a big hunk of driftwood and tosses it into the blaze. It slams into the white, glowing timber and sends up a shower of sparks. For an instant, the bulky sides of the trawlers, towering over them, are lit up. The faint glow makes the ships' masts look like long spears, thrust up into the black sky.

The cold north wind blew in our faces as we strode through the neighbourhood, jumping fences, running through gardens, taking the shortest route towards the shipyard. But we weren't cold; we didn't even feel the wind. We were hot and angry and ready for battle as we rounded the last corner. The big iron gate of the shipyard loomed in front of us.

'Look!' I said, pointing. 'There's one of them, guarding the gate.'

'Pretend you don't see him,' Roland said. 'Then they'll think they've taken us by surprise.'

We stormed across the half-lit road straight

up to the gate, and crawled under it. Then I heard that harsh, whispering sound again, and looked over my shoulder. A flaming arrow disappeared into the black sky.

'He's signalling them. They know we're here,' I whispered.

We slowed down and threaded our way cautiously among the piles of junk, ready at all times for an ambush. Further down, by the huge trawlers, the glow of firelight reflected on metal. We clambered over rusty pipes, between clusters of oil drums and past heaps of scrap iron, until we came to the clearing where the fire was burning.

Then they appeared. They materialised out of the dark beyond the fire: four black knights with grotesque bird-mask helmets. They advanced two by two into the clearing, and took a position a few yards from us. The biggest of them raised a sword.

'Welcome,' he pronounced in a booming voice, as if we were surrounded by an excited audience and this was merely a game. It was Eddie.

'Where's Manny?' Roland demanded, calm and concentrated.

'There's no hurry,' Eddie replied. 'You are here to fight, not talk.'

'We have to know if he is all right!' Roland insisted.

'He's just fine,' Eddie said, and I could see his wicked smile behind the mask. 'Are you ready to fight, Highlander, you and your little sidekick there?'

'Two against four doesn't seem like a fair fight to me,' Roland said. 'But maybe you're all just too scared to fight fairly.'

Eddie roared with laughter, and the others chuckled behind their masks.

'Oh yes,' he replied, 'we're trembling, aren't we, boys?'

They all raised their swords and screamed in mock fear.

'We want to see Manny!' Roland shouted.

'Get ready, men!' Eddie cried, without listening to Roland.

'Where is Manny?' Roland yelled in desperation.

Eddie advanced towards him and raised his heavy wooden sword. Roland stepped forward immediately, shoved his cape aside and brandished his grandfather's steel sword. Eddie stopped in his tracks. The steel blade glinted threateningly in front of him.

Jeff is breathing hard behind his mask, watching Eddie approach Roland, watching Roland drawing the huge steel blade from underneath his cape, pointing it at Eddie. *Maybe if I just run away, then no one has to know I was here*, his thoughts flash. *Who are my friends? With whom do I stand, anyway? Now's the time! Run!*

*No, I won't run. I can't. I'm with Benjamin. And Roland. Manny. I've got to help Manny!*

Suddenly there was a commotion in the ranks of the Black Feather. One of the knights grabbed the archer by the shoulder and threw him hard to the ground. Then he raised his black sword and ripped off his bird-mask helmet, screaming, 'For Manny!'

It was Jeff.

The leader was quicker to react to the strange turn of events than Roland and I. He smashed his wooden sword with all his might on Roland's arm, and the ancient steel blade flew clattering to the ground. Roland stumbled backwards but managed to raise his shield to fend off the next blow and draw his wooden sword.

I ran at the lanky knight with the spear and struck him hard with the broomstick, and his helmet went flying off. He swung his spear back at me and we fought viciously until the spear broke, and then drew our swords. Out of the corner of my eye I saw Jeff trying to force the archer to tell him where Manny was. He howled and screamed as Jeff hit him hard in the stomach and slapped his cheeks. Through the noise, the blows and the shouts I heard their leader roar, 'Keep your mouth shut! Keep your mouth shut!'

Behind me Roland and their leader were grunting and snorting as they hacked furiously at each other with blows that made their shields creak and crack.

Something heavy crashed down on my head, I saw a bright flash, and then everything went black. I didn't feel a thing when I hit the ground.

21

HIS ARMS and legs are tied and he sits huddled up inside an old van. It's their hiding place, but everything's been turned upside down, their things lying broken around him. He's long stopped crying and shouting, because his throat is sore and his voice is almost gone.

They grabbed him on the way to Roland's: black shadows that loped out from the trees, slipped a bag over his head and ran off, carrying him between them. When they took off the bag, he was in here. They've tied him to an iron bar that pokes up through the floor. He doesn't have a chance of freeing himself.

He heard them pile all sorts of scrap iron at the door of the van, and then their voices faded away and he was alone.

At first he had been terrified and had cried and cried; then he had become angry, wild with rage and screaming. Now he's just exhausted. He's been trying to fall asleep but can't make himself comfortable enough. Whenever he starts to doze off, he leans over to one side so the ropes cut his wrists and the iron bar presses into his back, jerking him awake.

Time creeps by, minutes, hours. No one comes, and he can hear no sound. He thinks of Mum and Tina, snuggling in the big bed, Mum perhaps reading a story. She thinks he's at Roland's and won't begin to worry before midnight.

Maybe it's midnight already? Or maybe he has only been here an hour? Roland and Benjamin are sure to go looking for him; they're bound to be here soon.

Outside he can hear the hollow humming of the wind and a cold draught is whistling sadly through holes and cracks in the old wreck.

I woke up with a terrible pain in my neck. I could hardly open my eyes, and I couldn't stand up. I knew the fighting was still going on; I could hear the sound of the swords clashing and cleaving the air, the panting and the grunting and the shouting. I opened my eyes and saw that Roland had dropped his shield, barely defending himself. Eddie was driving each thrust home with lunatic force. The archer had disappeared, but Jeff and the other one had abandoned all weapons and were rolling back and forth on the ground, punching, strangling and mauling.

He breaks free, jumps to his feet and kicks Jeff hard in the stomach, knocking the wind out of him. Then he runs off. Jeff is gasping, crouching on the ground.

Only Roland and Eddie are fighting now; Roland strikes hard with his sword but Eddie parries with his thick shield and the sword breaks in two. Eddie laughs as Roland scrambles backwards, looking around for a weapon.

Roland sees the ancient sword that has been lying there since the beginning of the battle. He grabs it and swings it at Eddie, screaming like a madman: 'Where's Manny?'

The sword is dangerously close to Eddie's neck and he freezes. He looks around and sees that the others have left. He stands still, breathing heavily.

'Tell me!' Roland cries, advancing closer.

Eddie throws his shield at Roland and runs up to the gate. Roland chases after him, but he disappears into the darkness, as if the earth has swallowed him.

Jeff crawled to me, touching my shoulder.

'You're bleeding,' he said.

Roland came running back and kneeled down by my side.

'Can you stand up?' he said.

I had a blinding headache and could hardly

move. Roland helped me to my feet and led me to an overturned oil drum, where I sat down. The wound was just a scratch and had stopped bleeding, but I had a lump the size of a golf ball on the back of my head.

Weapons were strewn around: a shield broken in two and the black bow lying broken and deserted on the ground.

I looked up and fixed my eyes on Jeff.

'What were you doing with those guys?'

'Do you know where Manny is?' Roland asked.

Jeff shook his head.

'They wouldn't tell me. They didn't trust me.'

'And you expect us to trust you?' I spat out in anger. Jeff just looked away without answering. Then he turned and started walking towards the gate. I was just about to yell after him, 'You traitor!' but Roland got in first.

'Don't go, Jeff. Please come back.'

Jeff turned around and gave us a long, sad look.

'I know you guys are angry with me. But I was angry too. Then I ran into Eddie and he had this idea of forming an Order. And I just went with it. I mean, you didn't care. You threw me out!'

'You threw yourself out,' I shouted. 'And we didn't think you cared, anyway.'

'I did care. I was just so angry, that's all.'

He stared at the ground in front of him and wiped his nose. Then he looked up at me, his lips trembling.

'I know you guys don't want me around anymore.'

Roland walked over to him and put his hand on his shoulder.

'We do, Jeff,' he said. 'But we have to stand together. All for one, and one for all, remember?'

Jeff looked down and nodded his head, still sniffling.

'Without you we would have lost the battle, you know,' Roland continued. 'You came to our rescue. Didn't he, Benjamin?'

I studied Jeff. I didn't want to forgive him

right away. He deserved to be raked over the coals a bit longer. I was sure he'd given Eddie the idea for the Black Feather.

'You told them everything about us, didn't you? Where we lived and all that, didn't you?'

He nodded.

'I told them you always had meetings at Roland's house. But then they went and took Manny. They didn't tell me about that. I didn't know anything until tonight. And that's the honest truth.' His eyes pleaded with us to believe him.

'We believe you,' Roland said. 'Benjamin?' He gave me a stern look.

'I guess so,' I mumbled.

'Now, let's get out of here,' Roland said. 'I'm sure they've let Manny go; after all, we met the challenge, and he's probably waiting for us back home.'

Jeff walked over to me and stood there for a while, hesitating.

'Friends?' he whispered.

I stood up and laid a hand on his shoulder. 'Friends.'

We grinned sheepishly.

'Come on, you guys,' Roland said. 'Let's pick up our weapons and get going.'

We gathered up what wasn't broken and tossed the rest into the dying fire. I was already looking forward to seeing Manny and telling him about the battle. And tomorrow I'd write a detailed account in the Chronicle of the Order of the Red Dragon. What a pity for Manny to miss out on our first real battle. On the other hand, we wouldn't have fought but for his rescue. On our way home we wondered if he'd be back already. Probably sound asleep, the lazy rascal. Wouldn't that be just like him? We walked briskly up the streets into our neighbourhood, feeling more like heroes than ever before.

22

OLD JOE tosses down his second cup of coffee and limps out of the shed to his late-night job at the shipyard. He reckons he'll finish it off before midnight. It's not that much anyway, just a pile of junk that he should have cleared away long since.

The bulldozer is waiting where he left it earlier, right next to the lorry, which will be driven away full of scrap iron early the next morning.

As he passes through the gate he notices the faint glow of a dying fire, in between the huge trawlers on the tracks. *Now what's that?* He shakes his head as he walks down to the tracks. *What have we got here? A broken sword! And a shield too!* He chuckles. *These kids, they're something else. In my day it was wrestling that mattered.* He shakes his head and limps away, leaving the fire alone. It's almost dead anyway, no danger to anyone.

He climbs aboard the bulldozer and releases the emergency brakes. The ancient engine groans and splutters, coughing black diesel smoke out into the cold night air.

*This'll be over and done before I've started*, he thinks, surveying the junk pile before him. A lonely spotlight, perched on a shadowy building, casts a blue-white light on the crooked iron, the bent steel pipes, and the rusty chrome fender of an old green van that's hidden underneath. Joe eases the machine into gear and begins the slow crawl toward the heap.

When we got back to Roland's house, his parents were still out. It was just as well, because they wouldn't have been too happy about him taking his grandfather's old sword down to the shipyard. We took off our capes and put the weapons away, and then hurried over to Manny's and rang the bell. His mum came to the door, looking puzzled.

'Is Manny home yet?' I asked.

'I thought he was with you,' she said in a worried tone.

We glanced at each other, but we didn't dare say anything in front of her. Suddenly my headache and fatigue were gone, and I knew something was terribly wrong.

'Well?' she said. 'Isn't he?'

'It's all right,' I said, acting relaxed. 'I know where he is, I just forgot.'

We ran up the street, leaving his mum with a worried expression on her face.

'They haven't let him go,' I said. 'We've got to talk to that Eddie!'

We ran as fast as we could in the direction of the big block of flats where Eddie lived.

It felt right to have Jeff with us again; it made us stronger. At last everything would get back to normal, as soon as we had found Manny. We ran into the building where Eddie lived, slamming the front door behind us and making a racket that echoed all over the hall, so Eddie the Bastard would know we were on our way.

Finally we were on the right floor, ringing the bell furiously and pounding on the door to the flat, shouting for Eddie to come out. The door opened abruptly and a large bear of a man, Eddie's father, filled up the doorway and stared down at us.

'What the hell is all that noise for?' he growled.

'We have to talk to Eddie. Now!' Roland answered.

I caught a glimpse of Eddie, hiding behind his father's back.

'Where's Manny?' I shouted.

'There's no Manny here,' Eddie's father blustered angrily. 'Get out, all of you. Goddamn racket in the middle of the night!'

Just as he slammed the door in our faces, I heard Eddie yell: 'In the van!'

We looked at each other, fearing the worst.

Our hiding place!

The shipyard!

He'd been there all the time!

We took the stairs three at the time and raced down the street. I couldn't even feel the pavement beneath me. Over fences, through gardens, between houses and across streets we flew, taking every shortcut possible to the shipyard, where poor Manny had been trapped in the cold and dark for three hours.

A while ago he thought he heard voices, angry shouts in the distance, but he's not sure now. He's numb and he can't feel his hands and feet anymore. His exhausted mind is finally at rest, and now he's asleep. In the darkness of his unconscious mind, he senses something bright and strong, drawing closer and closer. The vague outline gradually becomes clearer. It's a white horse. A unicorn! Its long mane flows with the rhythm of its gallop; its snow-white horn glistens in the dark. Four giant hooves fall soundlessly on the grey earth. And with each step the horse takes, the warmth increases within him.

A loud rumble echoes around him, now rising, now receding. Then a crunching noise surrounds him and the world begins to spin and tremble.

The King of Horses moves steadily closer, as if his world alone is the real one, and the rumbling and the tumbling is just a distant storm in an imaginary place.

We ran across the street, crawled under the gate and stumbled, out of breath, between the junk piles. Then we saw the bulldozer. But no, it couldn't be. No, no! The heap of iron had been loaded onto a lorry and the area was clear. Our hiding place was gone. The van had disappeared.

We ran to the spot where it had been; we whirled in circles, looking all around, but all we could see was bare ground. We screamed Manny's name again and again, but there was no answer, just the echo of our voices.

A lonely spotlight, high up on a dark

building, cast a cold light on our pale faces and the clearing around us. I shouted his name, my throat dry, my legs trembling.

Then Jeff gave a yell. We ran up to him and saw that the van had rolled over the low cliff, hitting the huge rocks on its way down, before plunging into the black water in the harbour.

I crawled down, slipping and falling on the oily, wet rocks, until the icy black water engulfed me. But I didn't feel it. All I could see was the roof of the van before me, partly submerged in water. I searched furiously for the door, diving down into the slimy water, kicking my legs, then catching my breath, screaming his name, over and over again, even though I knew he wouldn't answer. Never again.

He reaches the green roof in the black water. He dives down and thrashes about until he finds the door. He kicks it open, and then disappears into the van.

He gropes around until his hands touch a

jumper and he pulls it towards him. But something resists his tug. He pulls furiously, but the jumper won't budge, and his lungs are bursting. He thrusts his head upwards, gasping for air, and calls out to Jeff, who jumps in.

Together they grope around for Manny and find that he's tied up. Jeff pulls out a pocketknife and cuts the nylon twine, and Manny's body slumps heavily into Benjamin's arms.

They drag him out, trying to hold his head above the water. But his neck is limp; there's a cut on his head and a black clot of blood in his ear. His fingers are stiff and his pale face is dripping with oily water. His mouth is half open, and the lonely spotlight on the building reflects for a moment on his crooked front tooth.

23

JEFF IS CURLED UP in his mother's arms, his father pacing the floor. Jeff is sure that he's angry, that he'll explode in his face, hit him even. But nothing has happened yet. Jeff keeps seeing Manny's body lying out on the stretcher, still and pale. They piled into the police car and Benjamin cried and cried. He can't remember whether Roland cried. But he couldn't cry. Funny, he feels he doesn't even need to.

In the police car he couldn't take his eyes off the dashboard, the noisy radio, the double rearview mirrors and the uniforms. Each police-man had a shiny whistle hanging from his jacket on a golden chain. Their faces were calm and relaxed; one of them even gave him a friendly smile.

He starts to think about what to do tomorrow—maybe he'll go down to the beach, all alone, and look for shells? Maybe go to a football match? That could be fun.

His father crouches down beside him and takes his hands, very gently. His face is not angry at all. And Jeff, for the first time, looks him straight in the eyes. His father is crying.

'My son,' he sobs. 'My dear son.'

He's about to say that it's all right, that he doesn't feel bad at all. But then his father takes him into his arms and holds him tight, stroking his head.

'It could have been you,' he whispers. 'I could have lost you.'

And now, in his father's embrace, listening to his gentle voice, Jeff feels he wants to cry, needs to weep bitterly for a long time. And he knows, finally, he can.

24

BENJAMIN is standing alone somewhere in a green field under a clear blue sky, looking around him. He's been here before, but he can't remember when. Far away on the distant horizon are tall mountains. Then he notices a movement in the distance; a great white horse is galloping towards him, the hooves falling silently to the ground. As it draws near he can see that it's a unicorn. And on its back is Manny.

Benjamin calls out his name and runs towards him. Manny jumps down and hugs him joyfully.

'How did you find me?' Manny says.

'I don't know.'

'Isn't this the greatest horse you ever saw?' he says, smiling wide.

Benjamin wants to say something more, but Manny places a hand on his shoulder.

'Just look; I've got a real unicorn, the King of Horses. Everything's all right.'

Suddenly he's on the unicorn's back again, and the King of Horses rears up on its hind legs.

'See you later!' he cries.

The great horse lifts its head. Then it dashes off into the distance, carrying its light burden, until it disappears into the brightness beyond the mountains.

These are my very best dreams.

FRIÐRIK ERLINGS was born in Reykjavik, Iceland, in 1962. As a writer, screenwriter, graphic designer and musician, he has proven himself to be one of the most accomplished Icelanders of his generation. In 1986 he founded the alternative rock band *The Sugarcubes* with Einar Orn Benediktsson and Bjork before leaving music to pursue his writing. Fridrik has written and translated numerous lyrics, written scripts for film and television, as well as biographies and fictional work for all ages.

*Benjamin Dove* is already a canonical treasure in Iceland, and this edition in English marks the beginning of Fridrik's place in English-language children's literature.

Fridrik is currently working on a screenplay for the first feature-length 3D-animation film made in Iceland as well as lecturing on screenwriting at The Icelandic Film School. He lives in Eyrarbakki, a small nineteenth-century village on the south coast of Iceland. There the ocean and sky rule to magical effect, an earthly setting as close as possible to a writer's heaven.